Author

FRANCES, V.

CW00739384

THE DEVIL'S DEPUTY

Renewals may be made by personal application,
by post, or by telephone

34113 00039100

The Devil's Deputy

On that fateful day, the town of Ridge Pleasant forgot its name and became instead a gory battlefield when the bank was robbed and the popular sheriff was left coughing up blood on the street. Who would form a posse to hunt down the thieves?

Into the fray stepped the taciturn Duke Pitson, a professional gambler with a mysterious past. He had been wounded in the raid and his friend the sheriff was now dead. So it was that Duke took up his guns again.

But danger was all around him and friend quickly became a foe. It would be a struggle to the death before Duke, with all his gun-skills and determination could bring peace to Ridge Pleasant again.

The Devil's Deputy

Vic Frances

A Black Horse Western

ROBERT HALE · LONDON

© 1950, 2003 Vic J. Hanson
First hardcover edition 2003
Originally published in paperback as
The Devil's Deputy by V. Joseph Hanson

ISBN 0 7090 7257 0

Robert Hale Limited
Clerkenwell House
Clerkenwell Green
London EC1R 0HT

Typeset by
Derek Doyle & Associates, Liverpool.
Printed and bound in Great Britain by
Antony Rowe Limited, Wiltshire

ONE

Sheriff Jed Travers coughed blood on the rutted street of Ridge Pleasant and the horsemen swept on and past him. Slugs from their blazing guns peppered the fronts of the clapboard buildings, and the windows behind which the surprised townsfolk raised their own weapons for a belated retaliation.

Duke Pitson ran on to the boardwalk, his gun raised. He felt a searing pain like a red hot poker stabbing into his thigh and his leg went weak as water beneath him. He pitched forward on his face. For a moment he lay fighting the nausea that threatened to overcome him; through a haze he saw Jed lying like a dog in the middle of the street – and the hats of the riders disappearing, like so many gophers into their holes, below the rise at the end of the drag.

Duke let himself fall down the three steps from the boardwalk and began to crawl. His sombrero had rolled out of sight somewhere and the midday sun beat down on his tawny head. He left a smeary trail of blood in the dust behind him.

Men were running into the street now and untieing horses from hitching-rails or jostling with lurid curses to the rise and blazing away in futility. Duke reached the sheriff before anybody else did.

Jed lay on his stomach with his face in the dust. Duke groaned, his arms were weak, his fingers powerless; he slumped forward suddenly in a faint.

People began to gather around the two men lying in the dust. Nobody seemed to know rightly what to do.

A man came out of the *Golden Heifer Saloon* and down the steps, following roughly the trail of blood left by Duke. This man's clothes held him apart from the others in the street in their workmanlike or seedy habilments. He could even give the fallen Duke a few points in sartorial elegance. His black broadcloth was of the finest, trimmed with silver silk braid and large pearl buttons; his fine leather riding-boots were intricately tooled; his flowing four-in-hand bow was matched by the silver grey sombrero and the fringes of thick hair that showed beneath it. He was of medium build; lithe, middle-aged, with a handsome lined face.

The people parted to let him through. A man said: 'The sheriff looks bad, Mr Heinkel.'

The man did not speak but went down on one knee beside the law-officer, who had been turned over and now lay on his back, his grizzled face calm except for a slight stretch of the lips, his eyes closed. A widening splotch of blood was staining his shirt just above the abdomen.

Heinkel bent his head and pressed his ear to the broad chest above the blood-stain. With a slim hand he caught hold of one of the sheriff's muscular wrists. Everybody watched motionless. He rose, dusting off his knees, his face expressionless. He said;

'He's still alive but we've got to be mighty careful with him. Some of you go get a shutter.'

Four men ran off to do his bidding. Attention was

drawn to Duke Pitson as he groaned and began to stir. A second later he sat up. He was a healthy specimen with remarkable powers of recovery. His thick black eyebrows, so incongruous a contrast to his flaming hair, accentuated the unusual pallor of his square face. He held both hands over the hole in his thigh and blood welled sluggishly through his fingers.

Heinkel said: 'A couple of you get Duke to his room. Tell Goatee to put a tourniquet on that leg.'

Protesting that he wanted to know what was going on Duke was hustled away. He became quieter when they told him that Jed Travers was still alive.

They were lifting the sheriff gently on to a shutter when the news came from the bank. A scared young clerk, his hands streaming with blood was helped out from there. When he regained coherence he had a pretty tale to tell. The bandits had gotten away with thousands – he didn't' know how many thousands. And the manager lay with his head smashed; he was probably dead.

There had been no sound, no alarm given to the town until the horsemen blasted their way down the main drag on their way out. A hastily-formed raggle-taggle posse had gone out after them. But they had a hell of a start.

The clerk had gone haywire again: he was babbling abut the bank being full of dead men.

He passed out and they carried him into the saloon to join the rest of the casualties.

Fat Doc Jameson, for once on hand when he was wanted, came running down the street and went in with them. He was no more drunk than usual.

The mob led by Frank Heinkel, walking like a commander before his troop, streamed down to the bank. They found the manager lying with his scalp split open. He was, however, still alive and was rushed down to the saloon. The *Painted Heifer*, at times like this, was always a place of succour. It was always easier to get Doc Jameson into a saloon than any place else and both Heinkel's barmen were handy boys with a casualty. One bank clerk rose dazedly to his feet behind his grill with a gun in his hand. He was disarmed quickly: it seemed to take him some time to realise he was among friends. He had been hit behind the ear with a gun-barrel. His partner lay a few feet away from him. He too had been treated in the same way; he was groaning, beginning to come around. The bandits had worked quickly and effi-ciently and without undue noise – until they made their getaway in the blaze of gunfire which stupified the townsfolk. They had probably filtered into the town in the first place, singly and in twos and threes, and congregated on the bank at a given time.

Ridge Pleasant was a jumping-off place for the border and saddle-tramps passing through, or often lingering for a while, were no rarity. Trail-herds from Tucson sometimes came that way bound for Mexican buyers.

Travel-stained characters with hard haunted eyes and low-slung guns were no rarity. The townsfolk, including the sheriff, watched them come and watched them go, and let them be – that is, unless they started any trouble.

The bank was closed up and a couple of shot-gun guards left there. Heinkel organised another posse and sent them in the wake of the first wild bunch in case the latter had mayhap caught up with the bandits and needed some help. At this juncture Sheriff Travers' two deputies arrived on the scene from the other direction. They had been chasing a couple of horse-thieves who had busted into the livery stables the other night and took their pick of the bunch. They had not caught up with the men. Their chagrin was doubled when they heard the news. Things were certainly popping lately. They were very concerned about Jed and were torn between the desire to go see him and that of going out forthwith after the men who had shot him. They tossed a coin. One of them went in the saloon and the other got a fresh horse and led the posse out. Everybody else jammed into the saloon.

Doc Jameson came downstairs with the news that the sheriff was still unconscious. The way he was the Doc wouldn't give a guess about him one way or the other. The bank manager, John Mallibeau was coming round and moaning like a sick cow. He was a hard-headed business man, in more ways than one, and the doc was of the opinion that he wouldn't come to any great harm. As for Duke Pitson, his behaviour was in direct contrast to the poised and gentlemanly demeanour which had earned him his nickname. Doc said he was probably ashamed of fainting like a schoolgirl over a mere hole in his leg.

Jameson, particularly when he was three-parts sober, was a shrewd old buzzard. He was partly right about Duke. The tawny-headed man lay like a trussed steer, visualising his friend Jed Travers lying like a dog in the sun and the dust; thinking what he himself might have done and hadn't; cursing himself for being such a fool to get in the way of a slug, and for passing out in the street. He figured it wasn't so much the slug that had caused it as the sun beating down on his unprotected head. He was kind of attached to his black Mexican-style sombrero, he wondered what had happened to it.

Above all he was worried about Jed, the old-timer had gotten a bad one. Duke cursed passionately in the silence of his room. Laid up here with his leg in a mummy-case and at the mercy of that drunken fool of a medico, he couldn't get to do nothing or find out nothing nohow. He was trying to get out of bed when Deputy Gil Dowling came in.

Gil was a yellow-headed beanpole with a limp. He had had his hip smashed by a bullet during a run-in with some rustlers two years ago and rough surgery had made his one leg shorter than the other.

'Take it easy, fellah,' he said. 'Take a shot o' this.' He handed the sweating Duke a flat square bottle. The redhead leaned back and took a grateful swig.

'How's Jed?' he said.

The deputy pursed his lips. 'Purty bad. He's lost a lot o' blood. Can't say how he's gonna be.' He sighed. 'Doggone it, I wished I'd gone out with the posse 'stead of Brock. I hope they get on to somp'n . Don't seem nothin' to do around here 'cept count our losses. Purty considerable too I guess. I bin doin' some sloothin'. Old Josh at the stables tells me there's bin quite a few strangers ridin' in the last coupla days. A few last night an' a bunch this mornin'. A couple of 'em dropped the hint that they had to hang around to pick up a herd comin' thru from Tucson. I've only traced three who came in last night. They all took a room at Mother Callaghan's place. They didn't check out this mornin', but they don't seem to be around. The ol' lady only saw them for a bit an' her eyes ain't so good. She don't recollect anythin' about 'em 'cept they look like cowboys. Seems like there ain't a single stranger in town at all right now. Their hosses are gone too. They fetched 'em out o' the stables one by one an' naturally ol' Josh didn't suspicion nothin'....'

'Damn neat,' said Duke Pitson. '*Very damn neat.*'

It was dusk when two weary disgruntled posses returned *en masse*. The first bunch had lost all track of the bandits in the hills and while prowling around had run suddenly into the second bunch. A gunfight nearly took place before they recognised one another.

Whoever had engineered the bank robbery certainly had reason to crow.

When morning came Ridge Pleasant heard the news that Sheriff Jed Travers had died during the night. It shocked them out of their worry over the loss of their money. Except for the rank badhats who had felt the weight of his horny fists or had stood at the business end of his swiftly drawn gun everybody had liked the old galoot.

Up in his room at the *Painted Heifer*, where he had finally consented to lay up until his wound was healed a little, Duke Pitson heard the news in silence. He was a taciturn man at the best of times was Duke. A gambler by profession he had schooled himself not to reveal emotion, only by a lowering of his head did he show his sadness, shielding his cold blue eyes and the unholy light that suddenly shone there.

'We'll get 'em sooner or later, Duke,' said Gil Dowling, who had brought the news.

The big man in the bed, with the cap of glossy red hair and the incongruous black eyebrows which made him look like a musical comedy singer, did not speak. But the air of the room seemed suddenly thick with menace. When Gil got out in the passage he shuddered a little. There was something about Duke sometimes that gave him the creeps. He had seen the gambler in action too. There was a cold precision about him that was almost horrifying.

He had rode into the Ridge Pleasant territory from out of the South roughly five years ago and had gotten himself the job of head dealer in Frank Heinkel's faro-bank almost immediately by the simple process of shooting his predecessor when that worthy tried to cheat him. He hadn't killed the man but merely drilled him through the wrist when he went for his gun. As it happened Sheriff Travers was in the saloon at the time and voted it was a fair fight. It wasn't the first time the dealer had been caught cheating. Previously he had managed to throw down on the accuser and scare him off. This time he came off second best and, nursing his wounded pride and maimed wrist, left town forever.

A further display of sleight-of-hand earned the newcomer the job. He was a worthy, though larger prototype of his boss, dandified Frank Heinkel, and helped to lend more class to the place. And, old-timers averred, he ran the straightest faro layout they had ever seen. In a shirt of spotless white and an embroidered vest, his hair like a golden cap beneath the lamplight he dealt cards night after night with gentlemanly calm.

His assistant was a slim young man called Blossom who had drifted into town a few weeks after Duke and attached himself to the big man like a leech. When he wasn't with Duke he was out riding on his lonesome. People said he knew the gambler from way-back, maybe he even had something on him: though that was never evident from the relations of the two men, which were very friendly. Trouble was Blossom was just as taciturn as his boss.

Blossom went out with one of the posses but they lost him somewhere up in the hills. He returned after dark and took his place beside the dealer who was engineering the faro layout in Duke's stead. His lean dark face was as inscrutable as an Indian's, his glossy black hair unruffled. During a lull in the game he excused himself to go and have a pow-wow with Duke. What those two silent characters found to talk about was a mystery to everybody.

Even after five years very few people had got beyond the red-haired gambler's gentlemanly and sometimes deadly reserve. Frank Heinkel maybe, Deputy Gil Dowling, Jed Travers…. What people did not know was that the sheriff had tried to check up on Pitson when he first hit Ridge Pleasant. He figured that no man who was that quick on the draw could be wholly innocent. He had most probably got such proficiency by constant gunslinging. Maybe he was a professional killer as well as gambler. But the sheriff could not trace Pitson any further back than Phoenix, where he had fleeced three would-be sharpers in a poker game and, when they got awkward, disarmed them at the point of his gun.

His conduct in Ridge Pleasant was impeccable and, except for threatening a smart stranger every now and then who tried to pull a fast shuffle, he never had occasion to use the gun which always lay in the holster strapped to his thigh. In time the sheriff got to know the man better and to become his friend. The bond between the silent young gambler and the equally taciturn old-timer was hard to find, but it was there all right.

Frank Heinkel was a creature of habit. He did things with the precision of a well-trained soldier. It was his

custom every night after he had ascertained that the
saloon was in full swing to go for a ride on his lonesome. Ever since he helped to build Ridge Pleasant
eleven years ago this had been his practice and
except for rare occasions he never changed.

On the day of the bank robbery he gave his
nocturnal ramble a miss but the following evening,
after the funeral of Jed Travers, he went out earlier
than usual. The old sheriff had been *his* friend too.

Once outside the town he set his horse at a gallop.
Down the slope from the mesa and across the valley-
land which was like a shimmering sea of silver
beneath the moon. He plunged into the hills, following without hesitation an unseen trail of his own. He
came through to the other side and into another
valley, an arid waste of sand and rock and tortured
vegetation. His horse plunged on, going downhill all
the time. This was a route to the border seldom used
by man and, in the centre of it was the ghost town of
Sundown.

In the middle of the straggling collection of dobe
hovels and broken clapboard cabins which
comprised the ghost-town were the ruins of a huge
hacienda. There were many legends about this place.
It was supposed to have been built by a fabulous Don
or Aztec in the days of the *Conquistadores.* Indians
and Mexicans gave the place a wide berth as they
considered it to be haunted and accursed. The town
itself had been built by a bunch of prospectors who
found a deposit of gold there. Sundown enjoyed a
short boom, then the vein proved to be a freak
deposit washed there by a hidden spring. It petered
out, and the population with it, leaving the town to
the buzzards.

As Frank Heinkel approached it that night the

craggy pile, surrounded by the shacks like beings at the feet of an idol, looked eerie in the moonlight. Lights gleaming among the ruins would have sent any superstitious Indian or Mexican fleeing in terror. But the saloon-owner seemed to welcome the sight and urged his horse on faster. He pulled the beast back on its haunches however when a voice rang out in front of him.

'Hold it, friend, you're covered!'

The saloon-owner sang out his name in reply.

'All right,' said the voice. 'Come on slowly.'

TWO

Blossom said: 'I followed the trail o' them buzzards right out into the badlands the other side of the hills, then I lost it in the shifting sand and on the rocks.'

'Looks like they've made for the border then,' said Duke. 'It's a long pull, but they could do it with plenty of provisions and water. They ain't likely to run into anybody that way.'

'Accordin' to ol' Josh, who handled their hosses, they were travelling light. They wouldn't want to be hampered in their getaway would they?'

'Maybe they had some chow stashed up in the hills,' said Duke.

'Yeh, that's an idea.'

'Curse the leg. Here, help me out of bed will yuh?'

Blossom put his arm around the other's broad shoulders. Duke put his good leg out first and stood up on it. Then he lowered the other gingerly to the floor. He winced but it bore his weight. With the help of his side-kick he began to hobble around the room. He was well away from the bed when the door was flung open and Doc Jameson waddled in.

He stood blinking owlishly on the threshold and said petulantly, 'I might've known somethin' like this

was goin' on. Consarn it, Duke! you'll bust that
wound wide open. Get back into bed!'

When Duke did meekly as he was told the doc's
eyes became more owlish than ever behind his spectacles. He blew out a satisfied breath, heavily laden
with fumes of whisky, and waddled from the room.

'Durned snooper,' said Duke as the door closed
behind the fat man. 'You an' me are goin' riding first
thing tomorrow morning, kid.'

Many folks had noticed that the gambler never
called his assistant anything but 'kid'. He was
Blossom to everybody else. That was the name he
had given when he first hit the town and what his
other one was nobody knew.

After they had made their plans for the morrow
the young man went back downstairs. Duke had
another smoke, then, because he had nothing else to
do, went to sleep. The sounds of the bar room to
which he were so accustomed lulled him deeply.

When he awoke the sounds were no more. There
was only the deep quiet of the Western night;
through the window a cool breeze bringing a smell of
dust and brushwood. A sound had awakened him, he
was alert in an instant, his hand reaching up and closing around the butt of his gun, which hung in his
gunbelt over the bed rail. He realised that someone
was softly ascending the stairs. He cursed his
wounded leg, which would not allow him to get out
of bed without making a racket. The steps came
along the passage and without a pause past the door
of his room. It was then that, although they were
muffled, he recognised them.

Frank was late tonight! It was characteristic of him
that he was tiptoeing in order not to wake anyone.
He was a considerate sort of a galoot.

Duke heard him open the door of his own room at the end of the hall and close it softly behind him. All was silence again. The gambler wondered what had kept his boss out so late but dismissed it as none of his business anyway and went back to sleep.

As prearranged, Blossom was on hand just after dawn. He said the horses were saddled and waiting out back. Standing on his own two pins, Duke dressed and buckled on his gun-belt. It was characteristic of him that he thought of the latter as part of his clothing. He sat on the bed to put his boots on last. The wound was high up in his thigh so he had no difficulty. His only fear was that he might not be able to bend his leg around the horse's flank.

He rested his hands on Blossom's shoulder as they went as softly as possible down the passage. His high-heeled riding boots made walking difficult and his wound throbbed alarmingly. If Doc Jameson could see him now he would throw a fit. But the old buzzard was probably snoring like a pig in a wallow.

They reached ground level without mishap and went through the little back door. Blossom had to help Duke into the saddle of his big black gelding but, once he had his feet in the stirrups, the redhead said he felt a whole lot better.

'I've got to fetch some chow,' said Blossom and went back into the saloon.

He reappeared a few moments later with a bulging gunny-sack and a hat. The latter was Duke's sombrero.

'It had rolled under the piles out front,' said Blossom.

Duke clapped it on his leonine head. 'Better than ever,' he said.

They made their way along the backs of the sleep-

ing town and out on to the trail. Then they quick-
ened their horses' paces. If Duke's leg hurt him at all,
no sign of it showed on his brown square face.
However, he was sweating profusely when they
reached the hills – and it wasn't only due to the
morning sun. It was Blossom who, understanding his
partner's queer pride, finally called a halt with the
plea that he was 'durned hungry.'

They bivouacked in the shade of a bluff and ate
the sandwiches Blossom had prepared. They drank
half a canteen of cold black coffee laced with rum.
They still had two canteens of this left besides – and
one of water. Blossom was taking no chances of
either of them being badlands' buzzard-bait.

After a smoke they pushed on and Blossom began
to lead the way along the trail he had followed
before.

When they got into the badlands proper, the sun
was like a brass gong in the sky, its rays bouncing
from the hard rock and the white alkali dust. They
pulled their hats low over their eyes and their neck-
erchiefs up over their mouths. The very air seemed
to turn to dust on their lips.

Blossom said: 'Around about here was when I lost
the trail.'

He got from his horse and began to prowl along in
front like a hound-dog after a scent. At one point he
even got down on his knees in the sand. But, finally,
he turned, throwing up his arms in disgust.

Duke knew that if Blossom couldn't pick up the
trail, probably nobody could. With his thick black
hair, high cheekbones and lean dark face, he looked
part-Indian, and he certainly tracked like one.

They decided to push on further in the hopes of
picking something up. Little did they know how

successful, in a sense, they were going to be.

A heat-haze obscured the horizon. To look into it for only a short time made their eyes stream with tears and their heads spin. There was nothing to see but a seemingly limitless expanse of arid land broken only at intervals by small outcrops of rocks and stunted cacti. Above it was the shimmering yellow-blue haze of the sky, and the glaring ball of the sun which they could not look upon.

It was Blossom who first spotted something. He shaded his eyes with his hands and looked out to the horizon.

'Buzzards,'   he said. 'A whole bunch of 'em. There's carrion somewhere out there.'

They urged their horses to a gallop. The buzzards rose higher and wheeled away with shrill scolding cries as the horsemen got closer. A crumpled thing lay under the pitiless sun and already the sand around it had been scratched and pockmarked by the claws of the flesh-eating birds.

Both men dismounted and, walking awkwardly in their stilt-heeled boots, approached the bundle, black on the white sand. It was the body of a man lying on his side with his knees drawn up as if in sleep. His head was queerly twisted and one bulging eye was visible, staring sightlessly into the sun.

The two men got down on their knees beside the man. He was, indubitably, dead, but it did not look like the buzzards had gotten near enough to him yet to do him any further damage They were craven cautious creatures and had probably hovered above for some time, making sure the object was really a dead and harmless thing before plummeting any lower. Duke and Blossom had arrived just in time to prevent their feast. No wonder the creatures were shrieking, high in the distance.

Duke rolled the body over on its back. The bent knees, stiff in death even in the hot sun, stuck up grotesquely but, when Duke put his hand to them, they straightened out like the jointed limbs of a dummy.

The body was that of a long lean man clad in plain ordinary Western garb. Faded blue jeans with patch pockets, a thick leather belt to hold them up but no gunbelt; a faded black shirt. The latter was open at the top, showing the man's scraggy hairy chest. The head lolled backwards now, stretching the scrawny neck and revealing the livid purple weal around it, deeply furrowing the pallid flesh. There lay the reason for the contorted face, the bulging eyes and tongue bitten by yellow teeth.

'He's bin roped,' said Blossom.

'He ain't bin here overlong either,' said Duke. 'Since first thing this morning maybe.'

Silent again they stared down at the body, trying to read aright the mute story it told. The feet of the corpse were bare and so was the head, with the mop of black matted hair.

'Looks like the body was brought here an' dumped,' said Duke.

Blossom nodded silently. He rose and began to circle away from the area over which the buzzards had begun their sortie before they were interrupted. Already their marks were being obliterated by the shifting sand, so Blossom had little hope of finding anything else. He moved in ever-widening circles while, behind him, Duke went through the dead man's pockets. Both men were very painstaking.

Blossom returned. Duke looked up and said:

'There ain't a thing in his pockets. Looks like they've been cleaned dry.'

Blossom said: 'There are a few hoofprints out there.' He pointed, 'like as if a bunch've milled around. But which way they went I can't rightly tell. The sand is covering everything now an' a bit further on yuh come to rock once more…. I found this out on the rocks.' He opened his palm to reveal what glittered there.

Duke took it from him and scrutinised it. He said: 'It looks like a lucky charm of some kind; the kind of thing Mexicans have stitched on their clothes or horses' reins.'

Blossom said: 'It's a bit tarnished, but whether from lying out there a lot or for lack of care on the part of its owner is hard to say. Maybe it's been out there some time….'

'Or maybe it was dropped by the people who brought this poor devil out here….' Duke finished the sentence for him.

Then he went on: 'It's a queer set up – the man wasn't dragged here at the end of the rope – no marks on his body. He must've been finished off in some other place an' then dumped here….'

'An' they didn't even bother to bury him.'

'He wouldn't've been brought out to the desert from the other side – he must've been finished off in the hills…. C'mon,' said Duke, ' let's get the poor crittur on to a hoss.'

'You think maybe he was one of that gang?' said Blossom as he helped the big man with his burden.

'Maybe, who knows? It looks like the work of somebody who was in a hurry.'

When Frank Heinkel entered Sundown that night he

was met by two men, vague menacing shapes in the soft gloom. He spoke to them softly, part of the mystery now, and they ranged themselves one reach side of him. They walked with him in this manner to the walls of the ruins in the centre of the camp, then they left him.

He opened a small door in the wall, a door that seemed strangely new, that worked on well-oiled hinges. As he closed the door behind him a big man confronted him, a gun in his hand, his face shadowed in the soft lamplight. Heinkel spoke again and the man grunted a greeting in reply, allowing the saloon-owner to pass him.

Heinkel walked to the end of the passage with its crumbling walls and stone floor that echoed hollowly beneath his feet; he turned a corner and stopped before another door. He rapped this twice with his fist, then lifted the latch and opened it. He stepped inside the room and closed the door behind him.

It was more brightly lit than the passage he had just quitted, a large garish room with multi-coloured Indian rugs on the floor and hanging from the walls; a profusion of chairs; two couches; a wide desk.

Behind the desk sat a thin man with a narrow yellow face halved by a long black moustache. He said:

'Howdy, Frank.'

'Mancey,' said Heinkel briefly. He sat down on a chair with rainbow cushions, taking off his hat and his gloves and placing them gently on the edge of the desk. His hands were fine and thin, his whole bearing gave an impression of gentleness; his lined handsome face seemed that of a man who had suffered much.

With a nod he lifted the lid of the rosewood cigarette box which Mancey pushed across the desk. He selected a thin black Mexican cheroot.

The two men lit up and inhaled deeply. Then Heinkel said: 'Sheriff Travers is dead.'

'Is he?' said the other man, his voice a deep burr.

Heinkel said: 'Yes, and he was my friend. I told you no shooting if it could be avoided. You could have knocked him over.'

Mancey said: 'It was one of my men – an impulsive fellow....'

'I want him punished,' said Heinkel. 'An eye for an eye. The sheriff was my friend. You gave your word.'

'He shall be punished,' said Mancey. More and more like Heinkel, he was lapsing into cultured border idiom, a Don entertaining a distinguished visitor whose every word, in the custom of old-world hospitality, was law.

He rose and crossed to the door. He was not a Mexican, but about him there was something of the catlike grace of the finer people of that race. Maybe something of an Indian too as well as a gringo. Streaks of the blood of many races ran in Mancey Cole, but he owed allegiance to none.

He opened the door. 'Joe,' he called. 'Order some wine. And send for Peda Lomas while you're about it.' He closed the door again and turned back to Heinkel. 'We will wait.'

He continued to talk as he went back to his seat. 'It was a good haul, my friend.'

'I told you it would be,' said Heinkel. 'It's what we needed, it's what the men needed – but they must be taught to obey orders. Killing Sheriff Travers was absolutely unnecessary. You agree, Mancey?'

'Although, personally, the death of another

lawman means nothing to me I must admit that this time it probably could have been avoided,' said the thin man.

'I was against this job from the first, but I let you persuade me,' said Heinkel.

'It's done, my friend. It cannot be undone....' The thin man stopped talking as the door was rapped. For an infinitesimal moment he paused, his eyes meeting the expressionless ones of Heinkel, then he called, 'Come in.'

The door opened, a man entered, closing it behind him. He was tall, thin to the point of emaciation. There was a predatory look about his long face. At the moment his eyes were wary as he looked from one to the other of the two men. He did not greet Heinkel in any way.

Mancey said: 'Peda, you shot the man with the star on the street of Ridge Pleasant, and now that man is dead.'

'One less stinking lawman,' said Peda, in a perfectly flat voice.

Mancey matched this tone with his own as he said:

'My orders were, before we started out – no shooting unless it was absolutely necessary....'

'He was in the way, he was reaching for his gun....'

'You could have rode him down,' said Frank Heinkel. 'You could have even shot him in the leg.'

Pena turned on him, his mouth opening again. But what ever he had meant to say died in his throat as Mancey spoke again.

'It is agreed among the band that disobedience can be followed by drastic punishment....'

'Hell, I didn't agree to no such thing,' burst out Peda. He turned once more on Heinkel and this time he got his words out.

'I suppose this is your idea.' His thin lips curled –
'Trying to run a stick-up gang like a prayer-meeting.'

'By killing Sheriff Travers you've stirred up a
hornet's nest in Ridge Pleasant,' said the saloon-
owner. 'They're my people – I know them. Although
he was a lawman the sheriff was very popular.'

'Popular with you too, I guess,' sneered Peda.

'He was my friend,' said Heinkel for the third time
that night.

'So he got killed in a raid engineered by you, and,
because he was your friend, you want to put the
blame for his death on to somebody else – but all the
time you know it's yourself who's really to blame –
just as much as if you'd pulled the trigger of the
gun....'

'It's a lie – I was against it – I said no shooting....'

'AAAH – talk....'

Mancey Cole's voice cut in then. 'The fact remains
that you disobeyed orders and jeopardised us all by
doing so. You must....'

'You're not railroading me,' said Peda, taking a
step backwards.

Mancey's left shoulder shrugged a little, a gun
appeared in his hand above the table-top. Peda's
hand remained poised for a moment over the
scarred butt of his own gun then he let it fall. His eyes
were strained.

'A foolish thing to do, Peda,' said Mancey. 'You
know there is not one among you who can beat me
to the draw.'

'What're yuh trying to do?' said the other man.

'You will be taken out and judged for insubordi-
nation. If found guilty you will pay the penalty.'

'An eye for an eye,' said Frank Heinkel succinctly.

THREE

The arrival of the stage from Tucson was always an event in the lives of the people of Ridge Pleasant. This time it served to alleviate a little the anxiety caused by the theft from the bank of their hard-earned money. As many of them as could manage to do so were standing on the boardwalk of the *Painted Heifer* to see the coach come in.

It drew up in the customary cloud of dust and one of the guards jumped from the back and lowered the step so that the passengers could alight.

At this juncture another diversion occurred as two horsemen rode down the street followed by another bunch of townsfolk. The riders were Duke Pitson and his sidekick Blossom. Across the front of the former's saddle was slung the limp figure of a man.

The small cavalcade reached the saloon as the passengers were descending from the coach. The interest of the loungers was divided between the two spectacles.

A young lady took the helpful hand of the shotgun guard and descended from the coach. The necks of the loungers swivelled again and their eyes popped a little. She was a fashion-plate right out of a glossy

Eastern magazine, as pretty as any picture in her long gown and the little sky-blue coat, a perky hat perched on the blue-black curls that framed her roguish face.

Men doffed their hats to her as she passed them. A few of the older ones called her Miss Dulcie! Others were already moving towards the bunch around the horsemen on the street. She followed them with her eyes and then, impulsively left the sidewalk herself. The two horsemen saw her coming and both bowed courteously.

She said: 'Who is it?'

'Nobody you know, Miss Dulcie,' replied Duke. 'We don't even know him ourselves.'

'Can I do anything? – I took nursing you know.'

'Too late, Miss Dulcie.'

'Oh,' said the girl, her hand going to her mouth, her brown eyes wide above it. Then an exclamation from another voice behind her made her turn.

It was Frank Heinkel. He said:

'Dulcie! I didn't expect you yet.'

She took his hand. 'Uncle Frank! I didn't stay for lunch at Tucson – I came right along on the first coach I could get.'

He was looking past her at the group behind. He said: 'Go inside honey, your room's ready for you. I'll be with you in a moment.'

'All right,' she said and with a little smile turned and went.

Heinkel joined the group on the street, raising his eyebrow in query as he looked up at Duke. The big fellow said:

'We found him, just as he is, no hoss no nothin'. He was dead, the buzzards already beginning to gather. He's been roped.'

Heinkel raised his eyebrows high; he grabbed hold

of a handful of matted hair, lifted the dead man's head and looked at his face. His own face, with the silvery hair round the ears more evident as he bent his head became expressionless again.

'A stranger,' he said. 'You'd best take him down to the undertaker's. I'll come with you.'

The cavalcade, its ranks growing with every step moved on down the street.

Duke said: 'Pity Miss Dulcie had such a homecoming.'

'It couldn't be helped,' said Heinkel.

Little fussy Mack Dobbs, undertaker, received them with due ceremony and laid out the cadaver on one of his trestles, all of which were at the moment empty.

Frank Heinkel looked down at the bloated face and said: 'He looks a rough customer. Did you find anything in his pockets?'

'Nope,' said Duke. 'He'd been cleaned out.'

During the rest of that day and night the majority of the townsfolk of Ridge Pleasant filed through the undertaker's parlour and had a look at the new customer. But nobody identified him. More and more the two men who had found the body became sure that the man had been a member of the outlaw gang. But who had roped him – and why?

That night the faro layout was busier than ever but the two operators with characteristic perversity would not answer questions about anything else but cards – that is until, when the night was almost ended. John Mallibeau entered the saloon. The grizzled bank manager had soon got over the knock on the head he had from the bandits and except for the turban of bandages which hid his grey hair looked good as new. Behind him marched a bunch of townsfolk comprising most of the business men, storekeepers and such like.

They marched right up to the faro layout and halted there while the occupants of the saloon closed in around them.

Play was suspended for a moment, and Duke and Blossom looked at Mallibeau, the palpable ringleader, quizzically with their expressionless faces. The bank manager cleared his throat in his pompous way and began to speak.

'I am approaching you, Duke Pitson, for and on behalf of all my friends who are here with me tonight. They have asked me to nominate you for the post of sheriff of Ridge Pleasant and also to say now, before everybody, that if there are any other nominees for them to be put forward right now.'

The gambler's face was inscrutable as the bank manager held his peace for a moment and everybody else started to talk at once. The voices of dissent were drowned by those of approbation. There did not seem to be any more nominees either.

Mallibeau held up his hands. 'Quiet everybody,' he shouted, then, as the hubbub died he turned to Duke saying:

'What do you think?'

'You haven't given me much time to think,' was the reply. 'I'm highly honoured, gentlemen, but why pick on me? I'm a professional gambler not a lawman.'

A little smile crossed the bank manager's face. He said, 'You're a handy man to have in a pinch for all that, the only straight gambler I know. The old sheriff was your friend, I think he'd like you to take over his job....'

Jamesey Porter, dour gunsmith, chimed in with,

'Let's have your answer, Duke,' and a sudden volume of voices backed him up.

The gambler exchanged glances with his assistant, an unseen message seemed to pass between them. Then the red-haired man rose to his feet and looked around him. The talking died.

Duke spoke clearly and with his usual brevity. 'My friends, Mr Mallibeau's last words decided me. He spoke truth when he said Jed Travers was my friend. I had made up my mind not to rest until I had found his killer. For that reason I will become your sheriff, but I reserve the right to resign as soon as I think my task is finished.' He paused and looked at Blossom, then continued:

'Also I'd like the kid here, who has been my assistant for so long, and who you all know as a straight shooter, to be my deputy.'

'Certainly,' said John Mallibeau. 'Certainly.' Then he was engulfed as folks pushed forward to congratulate the two new lawmen.

Jamesey Porter said: 'We'll get ol' Judge Pattison to swear you in then everythin'll be straight an' above board.' He raised his voice, 'Come on, folks, drinks are on me.'

They all surged to the bar, Duke and his sidekick propelled along with them. It was at this juncture that Frank Heinkel came downstairs to see what the shindig was about.

When they told him he was not heard to pass any relevant comment, but later he drew Duke aside. He shook him by the hand and said: 'I'm sorry to lose you, an' you're welcome to sit in any time, you know that. Jed was my friend too and if I can be of any help you know you can call on me.'

'Sure,' said Duke. He was inarticulate, he fancied

that for some reason there was faint reproach in
Heinkel's gentle tones. The saloon owner had lost a
head dealer which for the moment he could not
replace and it would probably knock a hole in his
takings. Maybe if Duke had stayed on he could have
had all the time off he wanted for his sleuthing....
But if those were Heinkel's sentiments he did not
voice them.

Finally Duke said: 'I'd like to keep my old room
here if I can.'

'Certainly, Duke,' said Heinkel.

'Thanks. I'll get back to the table now and play out
the night. Then I will move into the sheriff's office in
the morning.'

He returned to the layout and Blossom joined
him. They had both had plenty to drink but their
trained nerves seemed to stand it well. The bank,
'bucked' by half-drunken townsfolk losing to Duke
for the last time, really cleaned-up that night.

Duke and Blossom went upstairs together and the
latter said good-night and went into his room. Duke
carried on along the passage to his own crib. A door
opened up in front of him and Dulcie, clad in long
shimmering blue kimono came out. She turned
towards him and said:

'Sleepy, Duke?'

'Not particularly.'

'Come in then and let's talk awhile.' She held the
door wider.

Duke hesitated for a fraction of a second then
went past her and into the room. It had not changed
hardly at all since the old times they had used to talk
here together. Could it be true that the beautiful
young woman whom he now turned to confront, was
the merry pigtailed lassy who had dangled her bare

feet from the bed and fired innumerable questions at him. That had been four years ago. It seemed like much, much longer than that. He said:

'It's rather late at night for me to be having a pow-wow with a lady in her boudoir.'

'You old silly,' she said. 'Sit down.'

He plumped himself in the old basket-chair which had always creaked under his weight – and still did it seemed.

She sat on her old perch on the edge of the bed, but her feet did not dangle now and they were not bare. They were clad in blue velvet mules with white pompoms like tumbleweeds. Her ankles were bare, brown as they always had been. Her legs were longer. Duke could see the shape of them through the stuff of the kimono. They were beautifully shaped, as was the rest of her, right up to the perfectly moulded face which set off the full red lips, the wide brown eyes, the glossy shoulder-length tresses of her black hair. He realised that the gaming-like kid whom he had called 'the little Indian', was now a poised and beautiful woman…. But how young still. How old would she be. Twenty – twenty-one…? He realised that maybe he was staring too hard and his sudden unusual confusion almost showed in his face. He said:

'Well, how were things back east?'

She pursed her lips and raised her eyebrows and said, 'Hum-m, fine. I took all they'd got and am now an accomplished modern girl – turned out to a pattern just like all the rest of them.'

Duke was smiling, lending his square hard face a gentle glow. With a little spurt of laughter she continued:

'It's grand to be back in the old place again. I feel different already.'

'In a couple of weeks time you won't feel different you'll feel bored,' said Duke.

'I don't think so,' said the girl. Then her face sobered as she continued:

'The things that have been happening around here lately haven't been boring have they?' She leaned forward impulsively, her hands clasped in front of her. 'Duke, I was so sorry to hear about the death of the sheriff – he was a grand old man. Duke – do you think these – people will ever be caught?'

'We'll try our hardest to catch them you can be sure of that, Miss Dulcie,' he said.

She pouted and fluttered her long black eyelashes. It was a bit of coquetry he had not noticed in her before. A bit of Eastern coquetry no doubt. She said:

'You hadn't used to call me *Miss* Dulcie.'

'You're grown up now,' he said.

'I still like to be called Dulcie by my old friends.'

'All right – Dulcie.'

They went on to talk about his new job. Frank Heinkel had told Dulcie the news when he came to bid her good-night before retiring.

'He's awfully sorry to lose you, Duke,' she said.

They exchanged a few more reminiscences and then the man, who still could not get away from a sense of mazed unreality, took his leave. As he opened the door she called him softly again. He turned and she said, 'Take care.'

She was standing up beneath the light, a figure of dark beauty which for a moment brought a catch to his throat. He promised he would take care, and, closing the door softly behind him, crossed to his own room.

As he undressed he was thinking about her, memories of the past curiously intermingled with thoughts of the present. Then, as he took off his shirt something clinked within it and he lifted the flap of the pocket and took out a little glittering piece of metal. It was the charm Blossom had found out in the badlands by the dead body beneath the blazing sun. He held it in the palm of his hand and it winked beneath the light. A small piece of silver which might mean nothing – yet might mean so much. And he was back in the present again – with a glimpse also of an uncertain and maybe terrible future.

The following morning Blossom and he were sworn in as official lawmen and Duke was handed the small bunch of keys which had belonged to Jed Travers. One of them unlocked the door of the sheriff's office. It was just as Jed had left it. He had been an orderly man and his papers were stacked neatly on his desk beside his ink-bottle and his pen. His pipe was there too and a little pearl-handled pen-knife with which he had been forever cleaning it. The knife lay open on the desk as if he had dropped it there before going out into the street to be shot down like a dog.

Duke Pitson, not normally an emotional man, felt a queer constriction in his throat as he entered the place. It was almost as if he expected to find Jed sitting there awaiting him so they could have another of their quiet chats.

Blossom was very quiet, maybe in the queer way he had, he sensed his partner's feelings. On a nail in the log wall behind the desk hung a gunbelt with the walnut butt of a Colt protruding from its holster. Duke crossed the room slowly, almost mechanically, drew the gun and hefted it in his hand. It was an old scarred weapon, they had brought it here and hung

it up right after old Jed's funeral. Duke replaced the
gun then he took down the belt wholesale. He flung
back the wings of his fancy gambler's coat and
strapped the gun around his belly, crossing the one
he already wore. The coat got in the way a bit so he
peeled it off. He stood there a two-gun man, looking
somehow as if he had always been that way.

He left his coat over the back of the sheriff's chair,
went to the door at the back of the room and opened
it. Blossom followed him silently and they passed
through into the cell block. Only then did Duke
speak.

'It's time these cages had some inmates.'

Walking behind him as they left the place Blossom
realised that Duke's limp was becoming more
pronounced. The young man said:

'Is that laig playin' you up?'

'It is kinda,' said Duke. Both of them realised that
he had been on it more than he should have done.
But for the fact that he was lying in a drunken stupor
after the binge of last night Doc Jameson would
probably be after Duke like a rampaging bull.

'You'd better rest it up a bit,' said Blossom diffi-
dently.

'Don't *you* start,' Duke told him. He began to walk
a little straighter but it was with an obvious effort and
Blossom could see the small crystals of sweat beading
his forehead.

The tow-headed beanpole Gil Dowling joined
them. He, together with his partner Brock Smith, had
volunteered to continue as deputy under Duke. Gil
was an old friend of Duke's and was tickled to death to
be working for him, but it seemed that Brock, a surly
fellow, had just taken his usual line of least resistance.
But he did not deign to show himself to his new boss.

Duke's face was becoming white and drawn. His thick black slashes of eyebrows stood out on it like make-up on the face of a clown. His two friends persuaded him to come with them into the saloon and have the wound redressed.

They took him up to his room and ignoring his protestations shoved him down on the bed. While Gil uncovered the leg Blossom went to get fresh bandages. When he returned with the necessary, Dulcie followed him into the room.

'I'll see to that,' she said. 'I'm a nurse don't forget.'

'Aw, no,' protested Duke. 'The boys can manage.'

'Let her,' said Blossom. 'She just wants somebody to practise on.' He dodged her mock blow.

She was clad in a white shirtwaist, brown skirt and low embroidered riding boots. Her head was bare, her black hair swept back from her forehead. She looked fresh and cool. As she walked towards the bed Duke contrasted her with the sophisticated miss of the night before. What puzzled him was that he was not sure which he liked the best. They were both tangled up with a freckled tomboy with bare feet. He said weakly:

'Your Uncle Frank might not like you practising on such a disreputable guinea-pig as myself.'

'You know Uncle Frank wouldn't mind,' said Dulcie. 'Anyway, he went out riding early this morning and he hasn't come back yet.'

She ordered Gil to get some boiling water. She began to peel off the old dressing.

'If you're not very careful you'll be left with a permanent limp,' she said gravely. 'You certainly ought to rest up for a while.'

Right then he did not argue with her, admiring the

soft gloss of her hair as she bent over, the gentle touch of her fingers bringing him sweet content. And, even while he wished his two deputies in some place away from there so that he could be alone with her, he cursed himself for a fool.

She talked very seriously to him and they backed her up. She told him that he must at least lie there for the rest of the day or pretty soon he would not be able to walk at all. At long last wisdom overcame his pig-headness and he agreed to do as she said.

Hours later, in the late afternoon, he was lying there alone when he heard Frank Heinkel go past the door and into his room. He wondered where Frank had been all this time – the dapper saloon man's regular habits seemed to be going all haywire of late.

FOUR

Darkness fell and the night-life of the town began to hum as the folk left their work and sought their pleasure. Horsemen thundered in off the range and Duke could hear the champing of restive hooves and the clinking of harness as the hitching rack below began to fill up.

The hum of voices and movement from downstairs became more intense with every passing moment, filling Duke with a nostalgia which he had never thought he would feel for such commonplace things…. A dandy sheriff he had turned out to be, skulking in bed on his first day while two of his deputies reconnoitred beneath the blazing sun and the other sulked in a corner somewhere like a naughty child.

Doggone it, he'd get up and mosey downstairs. Maybe he'd catch somebody breaking the law nice and handy.

He got slowly out of bed; his leg did not pain him so much but was hellishly stiff. He dressed himself and stepped out into the passage, careful lest Dulcie should be round and hear him.

He reconnoitred the stairs in safety but bumped

into Doc Jameson as he entered the bar-room. The little fat medico began to splutter.

'Consarn it, Duke. Miss Dulcie told me you promised to stay in bed.'

'I'm no hibernating squirrel,' the new sheriff said, 'Quit fretting, Doc. Come an' have a drink.'

Still spluttering wordlessly the little man allowed himself to be shepherded to the bar.

He was drinking Duke's health for about the sixth time when a double blatter of shots caused him to jump and splash the liquor over his shirtfront. He was allergic to gun-fire. The shots came from out front and all heads swivelled in that direction. Sheriff Pitson left the bar and although his limp was noticeable, he moved swiftly as he crossed the room. He had almost reached the batwings when they swung open and Brock Smith came in.

The deputy's usually dark surly face was white. He was hatless and his lank black hair hung over his narrow forehead. He was swaying a little and his one hand was up at his shoulder. He saw Duke and blurted out wildly:

'Sheriff, there's a lead-slinging fool out on the streets. A stranger. He shot my gun out of my hand then nearly broke my shoulder with the barrel of his.... He – he says he'll fight anybody. He'll kill somebody....'

Duke said, 'All right, Brock,' and went past him, easing his two guns in their holsters as he walked. Somebody was breaking the law damn sight sooner than he'd expected.

The batwings swung to behind him and the hum of voices died a little. He paused then took a few steps sidewards into the shadows. The street seemed deathly still now. Something moved up ahead and

Duke stiffened. But it was only a restive horse at the hitching rack. As far as he could see in the light from nearby windows the street was deserted. Evidently the lead-slinging fool was laying low and the sheriff was alone, a target if he moved out into the middle of that street.

Duke began to pace slowly along the boardwalk. The man might be in front – he might be behind. He might be waiting in one of the alleys ready to slug or blast the sheriff as he passed.

Duke's leg began to pain him again, rubbery beneath him as he walked. But it was not only due to this that his body was sticky with sweat. And despite this his nerves were ice-cold. It was like facing a man across the table who had a winning hand but this time he could not see the man, the expressions on his face; he was gambling blind and his opponent held all the aces.

The street was silent and still but Duke knew that eyes watched him. Which of those eyes held menace – and where were they?… He walked at a slow steady pace, his hands swinging gently at his sides just below the twin gun-butts; the right hand his own black pearl handled forty-five, the left old Jed's Colt of the same calibre with the scarred walnut grip. Somehow they matched very well, they were just the right weight; Duke's slight list to the left hand side was due to his leg – it was a focal point of pain, of steadily blossoming pain, he cursed it because it spoiled his concentration.

The boom of a gun tore the night into shreds, shattering the shadows and leaving them trembling as the man on the sidewalk stiffened in his stride then began to move faster. The sound had come from up ahead and on the other side of the street.

Duke placed it in a small honkey-tonk known as Pedro's Place. He swerved across the boardwalk and halted behind a post as other sounds came from across there and light spilled into the street as Pedro's door was flung open. A deep voice shouted:

'Is everybody yellah in this town? Ain't there no law an' order?'

Duke left the boardwalk and began to cross the street. The other man was now only a shadow suddenly motionless on the edge of the street. Duke began to walk slowly towards this shadow. His wounded leg seemed to be made of india-rubber, pain shot through it with every jolt of his foot on the hard-baked rutted street. He tried to forget his pain and concentrate on the figure which became clearer as he got nearer to it. He wished he could see the man's eyes, which would give him away before any movement of his limbs.

All the time at the back of his mind a warning was drumming; there was only one man before him but there were too many shadows and he hated shadows. Even as his brain flashed a warning the man in front of him dived sideways into the darkness. Duke went down on one knee, forgetting the agony, and his hands moved with the old lightning smoothness, smooth gun-butts in palms, thumbs slamming hammers as his body went forward. The night was full of noise and the slugs seemed to come from all directions. The man on the boardwalk by Pedro's Place screamed hoarsely in agony. It seemed like he had only fired one shot – but there were others to back him up, flame stabbing from the other side of the street and from a point somewhere behind him.

Pain seared Duke's wrist, matching the agony of his other wound. His one gun spun from his hand but he swivelled the other, fanning the hammer although each shot seemed to tear the heart from him in agony. Then he was rising, running for cover, and the air around him was full of flying lead.

He reached the meagre shelter of a water-butt placed for the convenience of horses. But he was on the darker side of the street, the shadows were deep here and his opponents held their fire, waiting for him to give away his position. His brain raced. How many of them there were he was not sure, although he figured three, but he knew now that the whole thing had been a put-up job. They were after his blood.

Who was after his blood that was the question? He could not see them – and Brock had said the lead-slinging fool was a stranger. If that was him higher up there on the sidewalk his 'foolery' had cost him dear. From where he squatted Duke could hear the man's groans, which seemed to be torn from the very guts of him, he sounded as if he had stopped a slug down there. It was a horrible way to die, and die he would if he lay there much longer with the blood spilling from him. That was the way Jed Travers had died, that was the way Duke himself would have died had those bushwhackers had their way. Somebody in this territory certainly had a grudge against lawmen.

The man's groans became louder, a harrowing plea in them as the blood burbled in his throat. Duke could hear his scrabblings as he fought against the agony. But the big man felt no pity. And as he began to crawl on all fours in the direction of the sound, his mind was washed, and his body taut and cold.

Lights began to come on in windows on the opposite side of the street. People were beginning to think the shooting was over but they wanted to make sure first. Duke realised he would have to act fast or he was in danger of stopping a slug from one of his own side.

The man's groans were becoming weaker, there was a rattle in them. He was dying. As Duke began to move faster he saw the man. His head was in the diffused light which filtered from Pedro's Place. Pedro and the greasers who were the regular habitees of his layout were evidently lying low.

Duke flung himself forward and dropped behind the man, keeping away from the head. The man tried to speak, his voice a gurgle. Then Duke saw the dull eyes light a little. They seemed suddenly malicious and the mouth opened wide. Duke pressed the muzzle of the gun against the body and thumbed the hammer. The report was flat, blanketed, there was no flame. The man twitched and stiffened, and the flame came from across the street, the louder reports with it as the ambushers opened up again.

Duke flattened himself behind the body and heard another slug thump into it. He saw a glint on the edge of the boardwalk and knew it was the man's gun. He watched the flashes. They had the range but were shooting too high. The front of Pedro's Place was getting a peppering. Duke's one arm was numb, the blood caking on his sleeve. He held his gun in the other hand and rested it in the crook of the 'creased' arm. He thumbed the hammer rapidly.

He thought he heard a cry amid the rolling of the shots but he could not be sure. He rolled across the body, ignoring the glueyness which pulled at his clothes; he reached for the dead man's gun, grasped it and rolled. A bullet smacked into a post above him and he realised that he was being flanked. There must be at least three of the bushwhackers he decided. The one this side had evidently been biding his time....

Duke flung himself for the deeper shadows. His wounded leg gave way beneath him and he finished in a cursing tangled heap, his out-thrust hand sliding on something wet and sticky. Bullets thumped into the wall behind him and the night was a screaming cacophony of noise as the others opened up in force. Duke wriggled along the wall on his belly while pain beat at him in waves. They had tumbled to his manoeuvre and were firing low. A slug chipped a piece from the heel of his riding boot. While he had virtually no cover he dare not retaliate. He was sweating when he reached the water-butt. He re-loaded the one empty gun.

The men over the street were still firing but the one on this side was silent. Duke worked the fingers on the hand of his wounded arm experimentally. They were all right; the wound was just a crease. He raised his left hand gun and fired across the street, the right one lax in his hand. He began to thumb the hammer of that one too as the other man opened up and he realised he had crept nearer. The man fired a group of shots then he stopped firing, but whether he was hit or not Duke did not know; he was probably playing a possum's game. The others opened up again and slugs chipped the barrel behind which Duke crouched. He was in a tough spot, they were converging on him from both sides....

A door opened across the street and a man came out. The bushwhacker on Duke's side started firing. The man went back, began retaliating from the shelter of the doorway, the bushwhacker had given away his position – Duke placed his one gun on the floor beside him, he swivelled the other one and thumbed the hammer as fast as he could, sending lead in a steady spray along the boardwalk in front of him. The gun-fire made his head sing, the powder-smoke stung the membranes of his face. And through it all was the phantom sound of galloping hooves. He turned his head and saw the horsemen and held his fire, and in the sudden silence shouted:

'Blossom! Gil! Over here!'

They veered their mounts and came across to him. Across the street the lead-slingers opened up again and the slugs came uncomfortably close. But Duke came out of cover as Gil yelled, 'We'll ride 'em down!'

They didn't give him time to expostulate but turned their horses' heads once more and rode hard. Duke turned and limped recklessly along the boardwalk, fearful of what the skulker along there might do to his pards if he did not stop him in time. He drew a shot that plucked at his shirt at the shoulder and gave him a breath of caution. He lurched sideways and the next one missed him altogether. Then he was moving forward, firing with both guns, his heart singing savagely with them – with the love of battle. The lust to kill was choking his breast, making his heart pound, and he felt that his lips were drawing back from his teeth like those of any other animal on the rampage. Only gradually, as if in a dream from which he was slowly wakening, did he realise that no more bullets were coming his way. He stopped firing, stopped walking, leaning against the wall trembling a little, pain reaching him again.

He could hear the clattering of hooves and see vague shapes moving in the shadows across the street. Then gun-fire broke out anew, fiendishly and the scene was lit by lurid flashes in which the shapes

were black squirming phantoms. Lurching drunk-
enly, Duke began to run.

He skirted the body outside Pedro's Place but a
little further on almost tumbled head-first over
another pair of outstretched legs. The bushwhacker
was sitting stiffly with his back against the wall. When
Duke touched him he slumped sideways. The sheriff
lurched on. The shooting had stopped across the
street; even the horses were quiet, he had a confused
idea that they had clattered off down the street a
short time ago. He wondered what had happened to
Blossom and Gil.

People were filtering into the street as he crossed
it. Over there was an alley leading alongside Mother
Callaghan's boarding-house. The old lady was probably crouching inside wondering if the end of the
world had come.

Duke's skin began to prickle as, both guns ready in
his hands, he moved into the darkness of the alley. It
pressed on him, black as pitch, full of a silence that
was more ominous than sound.

He heard the shots from around the back of the
buildings and keeping close to the wall, began to run
again. He stumbled and fell to his knees, cursing with
the pain and awkwardness which frustrated him. The
shooting went on.

He was dripping with sweat as he rose to his feet
and pressed forward again as the shooting stopped.
As he reached the corner he heard the voice of
Blossom shout:

'There they go!' … Then the two horsemen swept
past the corner and even in the darkness Duke knew
they were strangers.

He raised both guns and triggered coolly and felt
exultation as he saw one of the men sway in the

saddle then slump forward over his horse's neck. He fired again but the horsemen were already melting into the gloom, the hoofbeats fading, replaced by the thud of running feet coming nearer.

Duke called, 'Gil! Blossom!' and leaned against the corner and waited.

The steady thud of feet became plainer to his ears and he felt a great relief to know that both his partners could still move that fast. Then they were upon him and he said:

'You two all right?'

Gil said: 'I got a flesh wound in the shoulder – it ain't much....'

Blossom said: 'I'm all right – I think— How about you, Duke?'

'I've got a crease in muh arm,' said the sheriff, 'But I'm lucky I ain't dead meat – you boys happened along just at the right moment – you certainly saved my bacon.'

'We'd better get out in the open,' said Gil. 'Or we'll be havin' some of our own folks takin' potshots at us.'

'Yeh, that'd be just like 'em,' said Blossom scornfully.... 'Looks like them buzzards have gotten away....'

As the three of them began to move down the alley Duke said, 'They didn't get off scot-free.'

Gil said: 'They were holed-up here and they started to run when we rode down on 'em. They must've had hosses waitin' round back. Not knowin' this we left ours an' chased 'em on foot....'

Blossom said: 'What was it all about, Duke?'

'Durned if I rightly know,' said the sheriff as they moved into the main drag. 'Maybe Brock can tell me more....'

He paused then, for coming towards them was the squat figure of that very person, and in the van, some more drifters. As the deputy reached them the batwings of the *Painted Heifer* swung open, splashing the street with light and disgorging its clientele.

Gil said: 'You picked a fine time to come, now everythin's finished.'

Brock retorted, 'I was the one who bucked the galoot in the first place and nearly got shot to hell. He was a madman.'

'There was more than one of them,' Duke told him. 'It looked like a plant. They were laying for me.'

Brock did not speak and Duke raised his voice, 'Get a lantern somebody.'

The cry was passed from lip to lip and presently a man emerged from the saloon carrying a lighted hurricane lamp.

Duke led him over to Pedro's Place and the motley streamed behind. Duke took the lamp from the man and held it over the spreadeagled body. It was that of a big man with shaggy black hair and the beginnings of a beard. He had lost an enormous amount of blood.

'That's the one,' said Brock. 'That's him.'

'Anybody know him?' said Duke.

There was a murmur Seemed like the man was a stranger. Then an old-timer pushed his way to the fore saying, 'My eyes ain't as good as they useter be; lemme have a closer look at him.' He wasn't squeamish; he bent over, peering at the body through steel-rimmed spectacles. Then he said:

'Yep, I guess it's the same hombre all right.'

'What hombre?' said Duke sharply

The old man straightened up with a grunt, his toothless jaws champing ruminatively. He squirted a stream of tobacco-juice into the dust and said;

'I wuz prospectin' up in the hills about a month ago when I hears hosses comin' along the path below me. I lies low an' takes a squint. There wuz a whole bunch o' riders – 'bout a couple dozen I guess. Real hard-lookin' customers – a lot o' greasers amongst 'em. This jasper,' he jerked his thumb at the body, 'wuz ridin' up in front with two other men. I cain't mistake him. They seemed in a all-fired hurry – I figured they were a gang on the run for the border. They didn't see me an' I didn't bother to holler 'em.' The old man spat again and began to cackle.

Duke took his arm and led him to the other cadaver propped against the wall. Everybody else followed.

The lantern-light illuminated a bloody mess, all that remained of a face into the middle of which a forty-five slug had smashed.

The old-timer said, 'If you want me to identify him I caint,' and began to cackle again.

The body was that of a thin man. His clothes, smothered now in blood, were definitely Mexican-style.

Duke said: 'Grab hold of his legs, some of yuh, and drag him into Pedro's Place. Bring the other carcass in too.'

Not without some wonder on the part of the protagonists, he was obeyed.

FIVE

As they entered his place Pedro came forward and Duke said, 'That's right, you can come and have a look now, the shooting's over and the law still flourishes.'

The enormously fat Mexican blinked at this sudden invasion of his premises and his face went a shade yellower as he saw the two bodies. His eyes started when he spotted the biggest of the two. He pointed.

'That ees the one who started the trouble, Sheriff.'

The small group of men, mostly Mexicans or half-breeds who were gathered at the small zinc-lined bar at the back of the room backed him up in this.

Duke said: 'I didn't notice none o' you gents takin' a hand while all the shooting was goin' on.' Then he turned on Pedro once more.

'Lock the door. I want nobody else in here except my three deputies.'

At these words Blossom, Gil, and Brock, shepherded a number of disgruntled townsfolk outside. Pedro locked the door.

He looked apprehensively at the two bodies that were dripping blood all over the floor. Then Duke said, 'Set 'em up Pedro.' And everybody moved towards the bar. The fat Mexican's face brightened as he bustled in front of them, and with the philosophy of his race, forgot all about the bodies.

As they breasted the bar Gil said: 'That leg's givin' you gyp ain't it, Duke?'

'It'll keep,' said the sheriff curtly. 'It ain't soppin' with blood like your shoulder.'

'No, but your arm is.'

'Forget it,' said Duke…. 'Brock, let's have your story.'

As the squat dark-faced deputy came close, he was nursing his shoulder. He said, 'I stopped one too but it was only a flesh wound. The doc fixed it up.'

'How did it happen?' said Duke impatiently.

'Wal, I came in here for a drink. The big fellah was already here drinking on his lonesome at the end of the bar. Pedro served me an' a few more of these galoots an' while he was doing this the big fellah begins to bellow. He wanted servin' pronto. Pedro didn't go down to him right away so he came barging along. He skittled my glass from off the bar with his elbow so I told him he'd better pay for another one. He gave me a push unawares an' knocked me over. I got up an' went for my gun, figurin' I'd disarm him and run him into the cooler for a night.' Brock paused.

Then he went on. 'He was drunk but he was a damsight faster than I expected him to be. He shot my gun out of my hand. Then he nicked my shoulder. After that his shooting got wild an' I had a chance to get outside. He followed me, an' he was still shootin' as I ran across the street.' He blinked his little eyes as he looked around him. 'Wouldn't you have run?' he said.

Both Blossom and Gil smiled, and the latter said. 'I guess so, you couldn't fight him with empty hands.'

Duke said: 'An' you fetched me. Is that what they wanted maybe. An' if so, how did they know you'd fetch me?'

'You're the sheriff....'

'Yeh, he was yelling for the law when I came out. I guess maybe that was a signal for his partners.' Duke turned on Pedro again and swept his hand towards the bodies. 'Have you seen that man before?'

The Mexican shook his head till his dewlaps quivered. 'No, Sheriff,' he said.

Duke raised his voice. 'Have any of you seen that man before?'

His keen eyes raked the dark faces. They all shook their heads or said 'No.' Pedro said, 'It was the first time he had been in my place – I theenk, Sheriff.'

'You think,' said Duke disgustedly.... 'How long had he been here when Brock came in?'

'Half-an-hour mebbe....'

'It didn't take him long to get drunk....'

'I theenk mebbe he was a leetle drunk before he came in.'

'Hum-m.... Then where did he get it...? Or maybe he brought it with him.... Aw, he wasn't drunk at all, he was just acting that way.'

'It was a mighty good imitation,' said Brock.

The hum of the townsfolk could still be heard from outside. Somebody hammered furiously on the door.

'Who the hell's that?' said Duke.

Blossom crossed to the door and listened to the voices for a moment. Then he turned and said, 'It's Frank Heinkel and the doc – they want to come in.'

'Let 'em in,' said Duke. 'An' nobody else.'

Blossom opened the door. Doc Jameson bounded in first and almost tumbled over the two bodies. He uttered a mild curse and then looked at them.

'Nobody I know,' he said feelingly. He waddled forward. 'Gimme a drink, Pedro.'

Frank Heinkel, following him in, skirted the bodies gingerly, but his face was as inscrutable as ever.

'You ever seen those bozoes before, Frank?' said Duke.

'Can't say I have,' replied the saloon owner.

He was immaculately clad in broadcloth with silk braiding. In the face of the motley, and rather dishevelled crew he looked very cool and collected.

Duke said: 'We'll have 'em laid out in the undertaking parlour an' have another identification parade. The hardcases who seem to be hitting town lately seem to be that strange that they might've come from Mars.'

As he spoke his strong face was beaded with sweat and there was an unusual twist to his lips. Doc Jameson looked at him curiously. No matter how much liquor he had imbibed the little man never wholly forgot his profession. He was pretty drunk now as he leaned on the bar and said:

'Looks like I got some work to do on the living – you first Duke.'

'I'm all right,' grunted the big man.

'You don't look all right. Let me have a look at that arm.' The little doctor grabbed hold of Duke's sleeve and tore it. He said:

'Tell somebody to go fetch my bag. Here's the key.'

Blossom took the key and went over to the door and opened it. He called somebody.

The doctor turned to Pedro and said, 'Get some hot water pronto.'

'Si.' Pedro bustled off.

His head close to Duke's Jameson said, 'You doggone fool, you never ought to have got out of bed.'

Duke said: 'Yeh, I'll skulk in bed while people drop from the clouds and shoot the town up. I'm sheriff ain't I?'

'Take your duties seriously don't you son?' said Doc.

'I do,' said Duke and his voice was suddenly metallic.

Mancey Cole looked up from the desk as Heinkel entered. He said:

'Frank, I didn't expect to see you again so soon.'

Heinkel's reply was in his usual unemotional tones. 'I should have thought you would, after the botch your men made of last night's job. I said scare the sheriff, not shoot the town up and get themselves killed in the process.'

'Scare the sheriff,' echoed Cole. 'What did you expect them to do, creep up behind him and say "Boo"? It seems to me that sheriff isn't easily scared. He got Butch, and Lopez and Bruno…'

'And Bruno?' said Heinkel.

'Yeh, he got him while they were getting away. He died before they got here.'

'And what did they do; leave him in the desert for the sheriff to find like he found Peda?'

'No, he's buried. It's too risky to leave anything for the buzzards lately.'

'Peda ought never to have been left there in the first place. Damn carelessness.'

'I know; we've had all that over before.... The men are grumbling over your kid-glove methods. They think those three men shouldn't have been killed last night.'

'Do they?' said Heinkel. 'Those three men played it wrong and they paid the penalty. They stacked up against a man who was too good for them. Anyway, it makes their cuts larger doesn't it? I don't expect they're grieving much. If my orders were carried out properly there wouldn't be any mistakes. We can't afford any more mistakes. The first and worst one was leaving Peda out there for the sheriff to find. He might get to thinking and bring a posse out here....'

'Bring a posse in the middle of the desert to look for bandits!' scoffed Cole. 'Not him! He'd never tumble to this hideout. This is a ghost town, nothing can live here. Nobody knows about the hidden spring except the old prospectors and they're either dead or in another State. There's no gold around here anymore.'

'There's one old-timer who thinks there is,' said Heinkel. 'And he isn't in another State....'

'Who's that?'

'An old coot named Zack Mowbray. He still prospects in the hills. He recognised Butch last night – and told the sheriff so. He spotted the band passing through the hills about a month ago. It must have been after the Lincoln job....'

'So he could recognise others of us?'

'I guess so.'

Cole was looking down at his desk as he spoke, grimly. 'Seems to me there's a lot of cleaning up to be done and the first on the list is that damn new sheriff of yours.'

'If you kill him you'll have to kill his pardners.'

'It can be done.'

'If it's done at all, it's gotta be done properly,' said Heinkel. 'No mistakes this time. Wait till I give the word.' He rose.

'Just as you say, Frank,' said Mancey Cole softly.

Zack Mowbray came out of the livery stables leading his cayuse and his burro. These three old stagers trundled along the street chewing rhythmically, the human member of the trio squirting juice from time to time. He walked a little in front, holding the reins of the horse and the lead-rope of the burro in one gnarled hand. The cavalcade was as old and as grey and as wrinkled as the arid country to which it belonged.

Zack drew to a gentle halt outside the stores and his four-footed friends followed his example; he was their mind, their creed. The old man passed into the soft gloom of the building and they waited patiently, ruminating, with slowly working jaws on things more profound than the ages.

The stores were next door to the *Painted Heifer* and were actually part of it and belonged to Frank Heinkel too. They were presided over by an ancient called Goatee Matthews, who was a sort of father-confessor to the town. His nickname was derived from the fact that he wore a moustache and imperial in the manner of the old soldiers and scouts, and although they were now snow-white, he always kept them perfectly groomed. He was probably even older than Zack and was the old prospector's only confidant.

'Off again, Zack?' he said as his friend entered.

'Yep,' was the reply. 'I've had my bellyful of town for a bit, lotta yammerin' and shootin' an' runnin' about. I'm makin' for the spaces where a man can have peace for a quiet smoke an' a think – an' the air don't stink of rotgut and powder fumes.'

'You always was a doggoned idealist, Zack,' said Goatee with a smile. 'What would yuh do with a pot of gold if you found it? I guess you're happier just lookin'.'

'Mebbe you're right,' said Zack. 'It is man's curse to search and reach for the stars. We all have our dream – our pot of gold, which likely as not will turn to ashes in our fingers when we find it.'

'Yuh durn' tootin',' said Goatee with a would-be sage wag of his head. Despite his romantic appearance he was a very practical man. This gave him great understanding but did not always allow him to follow his old friend's flights of fancy.

He said: 'Where yuh goin' this time?'

'Jest up in the hills to the north – by the Sugar Loaf…'

'You rant about the old place but you never seem to mosey far away from it.'

Zack leaned confidentially over the counter in the soft gloom of the shop, and with the love of mystery which was also characteristic of his old soul, lowered his voice in a conspiratorial murmur and said:

'Between me an' you, old friend, I found a small vein under the Sugar Loaf – mebbe it'll lead to something bigger….' He cackled suddenly. 'Mebbe even a pot of gold.'

'What do you want with a pot of gold, yuh ol' goat?' said the other oldster. He joined his laughter to that of his friend's. It was a huge joke. Zack always had news of a big haul but it never came off in reality.

They quit their sniggering when Brock Smith

entered the place. The deputy's dark face was as blank and surly as ever. He did not even smile. He strode to the counter and said:

'Gimme a can of beans, old-timer.'

'This hombre lives on beans,' said Goatee, as he handed over the commodity and took the deputy's money.

'How's the sheriff?' said Zack.

'He's all right,' replied Brock. 'He's tough.'

'He suttinly is,' said Goatee.

'Adios,' said the deputy and left.

'Queer cuss,' was Zack's verdict as the man's steps faded.

'Some folks say the same about you,' his friend told him.

'Mister Matthews, I take that as a personal insult....'

'What else'll yuh take?'

'A dozen cans o' beans. A large side o' thet salt pork. A can o' cawfee. Four pound o' them corn-pone biscuits. Some chewin' baccy....'

Zack paused. Goatee began to read the stuff back to him and as he did so, Brock Smith entered the place again. Goatee looked up, but he finished his spelling. Brock waited, then he said:

'I forgot to ask yuh for some makings, Goatee.'

'You're hazed,' said the oldster with a grin. 'Here y'are.' He passed across a packet of tobacco and papers. Brock took them, said thanks. Then he turned to Zack

'Goin' a long ways away, old-timer?'

'Purty,' replied Zack non-committally.

'You've ordered enough chow for a trip tuh Texas,' said Brock and a little smile lit his dark eyes for a moment then faded.

''Them dumb critturs I take with me eat an awful lot,' said Zack.

'Good huntin',' said Brock and once more he quitted the stores.

Zack had all his purchases put in a huge gunnysack and a few moments later bade Goatee a laconic farewell and set out.

People watched him and his beloved 'dumb critturs' go down the cart-rutted main drag of Ridge Pleasant and out on to the dusty sun-washed trail. A few waved to him and he nodded in return. Others ignored him – 'there was that crazy old coot off again.'

For himself Zack didn't give a damn for what any of them thought. They called him queer – let 'em! Doggone it if he wouldn't make a strike this time just to show 'em. He was pretty sure that there was rich pickings behind that vein of ore in the Sugar Loaf.

As he was riding out Frank Heinkel passed him on the trail and said:

'Off again, Zack?'

'Yup.'

'Well I wish you luck.'

'Thanks, Frank. *Hasta la vista.*'

'*Haste la vista.*' said Heinkel.

With a wave of their hands, the laconic salutation of taciturn men, they passed on their separate ways.

A real gent, Frank Heinkel…. Giddup you four-footed critturs!

Zack Mowbray and his friends pressed on into the sun, the shimmering haze, and the hills on the horizon squatting like a row of wriggling gophers.

SIX

Dusk was falling when Sheriff Duke Pitson came downstairs and limped across the bar-room of the *Painted Heifer*. His leg did not pain him now but the limp was very annoying and slowed him up quite considerably. It was too early yet for a big trade but there were a few folks clustered about at the tables taking chow. Duke went across to the bar, ordered a straight rye, double, and asked the barman if he had seen ol' Zack Mowbray. The man said he hadn't but he passed the word around. Somebody said they thought the ol' coot had lit out.

Duke finished his drink and went down the street to his office. Blossom, Gil and Brock were already there. They asked him how his leg was and he said fine. From Brock he elicited the information that the old prospector had indeed taken a pasear. Brock told him of how he had met Zack in the stores just before he left.

'Come on, we'll go down there,' said Duke. 'It's just like the old goat to light out now, he might've known I wanted to ask him some more questions.'

He told Blossom and Gil to stay put while he and Brock went down to the stores. The surly deputy seemed a mite more amicable today. He was kind of a hard hombre to figure. But Duke himself was no open book. Men spoke as they found in this town on the edge of the badlands. It was bad manners, and might prove dangerous also, to ask too many questions. Like Duke and Blossom, and scores of others of the younger section of the community, Brock had drifted into this mushroom town a few years ago. Sheriff Travers had trusted him and pronounced him to be a handy man in a pinch.

The two men confronted Goatee and the sheriff asked the old store-keeper if he knew where Zack Mowbray was heading for.

Goatee was uncertain. He liked Duke – in any capacity. He could not tell a downright lie; Duke knew that he was Zack's friend and the only recipient of his confidences. But Zack wouldn't want him to blab.

'If you know where he's gone, Goatee, spill it,' said Duke. 'He may be able to help me a lot in the case I'm working on now – an' you know what that is.'

'Yep,' said Goatee and made up his mind…. 'He'll be up around the Sugar Loaf.'

'Thanks,' said Duke. 'When I see Zack I'll explain to him why you told me.'

'You do that,' said the bearded store-keeper, his face wrinkled more than ever with anxiety.

The two men went outside and the sheriff said to his deputy, 'Go tell the boys to get their horses saddled, we'll ride out there pronto.'

'All of us?' said Brock.

'Yeh, all of us…. I'll meet yuh in five minutes time.' Duke went into the *Painted Heifer*.

When he came out again the three boys were waiting for him and Blossom held the sheriff's horse.

The moon was rising as the quartet rode out on to

the trail, a little wind soughed – then whipped at them in retaliation as they set their horses at a gallop.

'Sugar Loaf up ahead, boys,' said Zack to his two friends.

They being only 'dumb critters', did not pass any remarks. Maybe that was why he was so fond of them. They didn't give a fellow a length of jaw at the slightest provocation like some humans he could mention.

'I guess we'll camp here, you freaks, the Sugar Loaf ain't gonna git up an' walk during the night. I guess that big vein has been there a good many years – mebbe thousands, an' another night ain't gonna make it grow none – though I guess there'll be plenty enough for us whether or not.'

The knock-kneed burro gave a long deep sigh.

'Them's entirely my sentiments, Caesar,' said the old man.

In his youth Zack had been quite a scholar. In memory of those magical times, he called his burro Caesar and his cayuse Plato. The latter creature was indeed somewhat of a philosopher. He was silent; he did not seem to be at all excited at the prospects of a lucky strike. The open sky above him and a belly full of oats was all he desired from life.

The stars were beginning to wink in a blue vault and the breeze was cool when they made their camp in a little tree-fringed cup of land on the edge of the hills. Zack lit a fire, and when he could see it was under way, fed his philosophic friends, who were standing dejectedly as if on the point of collapse.

'Do yuh figure you've earned this, yuh lazy good for nothin' rapscallions?' he said.

To the sound of champing jaws he brewed himself some coffee and had a light supper of corn biscuits.

Then he rolled himself in his blankets with his stockinged feet toward the dying fire. He slept soundly, like a creature of the wild, knowing that his keenly developed senses would waken him on an instant if need be.

It was a nicker from his horse that awakened him in the stillness of the night. He sat up, his hand closing round the butt of the old Navy Colt which he always kept near him. He could hear no sound now but the whipping of the wind, even the horse had gone silent as if listening too. But Zack was aware somehow that there were other folks in the vicinity.

He lay down again and rolled over on his stomach. Then he began to wriggle from between the blankets, his lean old form becoming almost snake-like during the process. He almost buried himself in the grass, although it was stunted and brittle. He passed through a clump of parched tangled shrubs and rolled over the rise and into cover. He waited.

His eyes were just above the level of the rise as he watched the gloomy tangle of the trees opposite. The shadows broke and became pieces of moving darkness. The horse nickered again and a man cursed in a savage whisper.

'Hold it, friend,' said Zack. 'Stay right where you are.'

The night exploded; the shadows were shattered and became alive in flame. Gun-fire rolled on up into the hills. Dust was kicked up into Zack's nostrils, but the smell of it was not half so good as that of his own powdersmoke as he saw one of the men go down and heard his shrill screaming. He winced as a hot breath stung his cheek, then the black shadows were part of the trees once more and he was wriggling backwards seeking better cover.

He reached loose shale and it rattled beneath him. He flopped on his stomach as the gun-fire started again. He felt like a lizard pinned there as the slugs whistled over him and smacked into the rocks. A mite lower and he'd be cold turkey. There came a lull in the firing and he knew that next time they would have the range. It was a split second of grace and he took it and acted, throwing himself forward desperately to a shadowy cleft in the rocks.

Bullets whistled and ricocheted around him and as he negotiated the corner he almost cried out in agony as a red-hot fang bit into his ankle. Then, sweating and trembling, he was crouched in cover, his knees drawn up almost to his chin. He put his hand down to his ankle, which was burning and useless, and it came away wet and sticky. His teeth were on edge with the feel of brittle bone and pulped flesh, and he knew that even if he had a chance to run he wouldn't be able to any more.

The smooth sides of boulders seemed to be all around him except for at the opening of the cleft. The corner hid him from the trees and he could shoot around it. He was safe for the moment. But how long could he last that way? He did not know how many men he was up against or whether there were any more apart from those in the trees. Four maybe there, he had figured; one he had put paid to…. Whoever they were, why were they after him? Just wandering hardcases, greasers maybe, who'd kill a man for his boots. Zack grinned wryly; well, if it was pickings they were after they'd come a mite too early to get anything out of him. Now, if he was on his way back maybe….

The gun-fire broke out afresh, savage, as if it would tear him from his hiding-place with its very violence.

Bullets smacked into the rocks all around him, they whined and boomed, awakening the echoes of the hills. Chips stung his face and dust blew into his eyes but he was well covered in his little box. He peeped cautiously around the corner as the firing died, and from a belated flash, picked up the position of his opponents. He squinted, and thumbed the hammer of his Navy Colt.

The gun bucked in his hand as it sang and the pain he was in was for a moment like pleasure. Then the gun was empty and he reloaded furiously, cursing that he had omitted to bring his rifle, which had been near his hand too…. Still, he hadn't expected anything like this!

For a moment he felt a sense of frustration, a gloomy foreboding that was alien to his nature but in his philosophy he could not deny. Was it ordained that he should be destroyed here when he was almost at the end of his search? *What search? What end?* Had he not been as happy as any man had a right to be and was not 'the end' maybe just a continuation of that happiness? Maybe his pot of gold was only ashes after all and he would be far better off if he never found it. So his frustration became a sweet philosophy.

A sudden shaft of pain made him feel like howling, and being reminded of his wound, he realised that even if he did get out of this hole he could not get far on a busted ankle.

It was just like him to philosophise while in a tight corner; his old age had not brought him sense…. But even as his mind worked he was alert and he heard his opponents begin to move. *Trying to creep up on him were they?* He elevated his Colt and let fly once more and this time was rewarded by the sound of a groan.

There was a scuffle and then they started to retaliate.

The slugs came perilously close this time, and as he flattened himself against the rocks, he realised they had gotten nearer and into a better position for shooting at him. He could not move and they could.

He dragged himself along to the back of the cleft. Every movement sent stabs of pain through his leg. Grunting, he raised himself on to his knees, his hands reaching upwards. The rock-face here was uneven and sloping. Here maybe was an outlet he had not expected to find. If he could make it!

He reached up as high as he could, found crevices with his fingers and hauled himself up. Pain flamed through his body and he felt sweat breaking out all over him. His wounded ankle and the leg above it was like a dead weight holding him back. He hung in mid-air for a moment, his good foot scrabbling for a hole. The sound was terribly loud in the stillness and was followed almost immediately by the blast of the guns. Lead sang close, and hanging perilously by one hand, he turned and retaliated. Then, ignoring the pain as his smashed ankle bumped against the rocks, he began to climb faster.

The shots were a barrage which dinned his ears. They seemed to be all around him and much nearer now.

The shooting ceased and he heard the sound of movement; the night was full of them and they were all around him too. Then the shooting started again, the flames lighting the darkness around him – and up above him too. Looking up he felt the close breath of the slugs, and hanging by one hand once more, his nails digging into the rock-face he raised his gun and fired back.... fired rapidly, madly, until the powder-smoke choked him and the pain blinded him....

*

Sheriff Pitson and his three deputies heard the shots from afar, like echoes from another sphere. They spurred their horses on faster; the wind whipped at them, carrying the sounds away so that it was hard to determine their precise direction. Finally they halted to listen.

'We must have been imagining things,' said Gil after a bit.

But no sooner were the words out of his mouth than Blossom said, 'Listen, there it goes again!'

Duke said: 'I figure it's pretty near to where we're heading. Come on!'

As the crackle of gun-fire died again into the wind, they galloped madly, and in all their minds was the thought of Zack Mowbray.

They had reached the edge of the better grass when the shooting came to them again, even above the drumming of their horses' hooves and the rush of the wind. The ground, sandy and sparsely grassed now, was beginning to rise a little.

'Over there!' yelled Duke as the slopes of the hills were lit intermittently by gun-flashes.

They drew their guns as they forced their horses upwards. The firing died.

When it started up again they realised it was aimed at them. 'Split up!' yelled Duke.

They fanned out, then, at a sudden sign from their leader, slowed down a little. Above the sound of their own horses' hooves they heard others. 'They're making a run for it!' yelled Duke and spurred his mount to greater efforts.

More shots came, and above them, in the brief flashes, they saw the silhouettes of horsemen. They began to retaliate. They climbed a tortuous rocky way in the darkness – perilously, while their quarry took pot-shots at them from time to time. Blossom's horse screamed in terror as a slug stung its neck. It reared and he was hard put to control it. His pards held their fire and finally the cayuse became quieter. The other people's defiant shots were falling short as they drew farther away.

'They must know these hills a damn sight better than we do,' said Gil. 'They're travelling at a hell of a rate.'

They reached the top of a rise and halted, listening. Up ahead of them hooves beat hollowly on rock, the echoes spectral, fading all the time.

'I reckon its purty hopeless,' said Duke. 'We'll never catch 'em now.'

The other three men reluctantly agreed with him. They turned their horses' heads.

Blossom said: 'I figure that, in the first place the shots came from somewhere down there.' He pointed with a slim gloved hand in the darkness.

'Lead the way,' said Duke.

The nicker of a horse led them finally to a hollowed clearing at the rocky base of the hills. A clearing surrounded by stunted vegetation. Beside the drooping raw-boned cayuse they found a burro lying on its side. It had stopped a bullet but was still panting feebly. The men dismounted. Duke put a bullet through the suffering creature's brain.

'They're Zack's animals,' said Brock.

Moseying around the trees Blossom suddenly called out. 'Here's a body – deader than a coffin lid. Shot in the guts.'

Gil discovered the ashes of the fire, Zack's gunney-sack full of provisions, his blanket, his hat and his rifle. Then, past there, Brock found another body.

'Looks like they tried to jump Zack an' he put up a helluva fight,' said Duke.

'He would,' said Blossom. 'If there was anything that ol' buzzard lacked it wasn't guts.'

'Looks like they were movin' this way,' cried Brock. 'Zack must've been makin' for the rocks.'

The other three joined him, expressing the wish that the old-timer had gotten away after all. They climbed the rocks and found another dead body atop of them. It was lying on its stomach, a gun still clutched in one hand, the other clawing at the rock-face. They rolled the body over and discovered the man had been shot in the throat. He was lying on the edge of a lip of rock. There was a dark fissure below him.

It was the agile Blossom who descended the rocky slope and after a bit of feeling around, cried:

'Zack's down here.' The other three joined him and Duke struck a match.

The old prospector was lying on his back. His lined face was composed, there was an almost kindly look upon it. His eyes were closed. A single bullet had entered his chest. He must have died pretty quickly. His one hand was across his body, just below the wound and his old Navy Colt was clasped within it.

The four men doffed their hats. They were silent. Ranting would do no good, it would seem sacrilege in this shrine, in the face of a tale of such carnage. Many cashed in their chips this way in the lawless West. But that did not make Zack Mowbray's long battle any less noble. They could only wonder why this should happen to an old man who, though many called him queer, had never done harm to anyone.

Finally Duke broke the silence, saying softly, with a weight of sadness, 'Well, we found him an' I guess there's nothing more we can do now. We'd better pack him on his horse and take him back to town.'

SEVEN

The people of Ridge Pleasant heard the news of Zack Mowbray's death with mixed feelings. The general feeling at first was of wonder but this changed in some subtle way and became an almost universal one of sadness.

Many who had thought him queer began to recollect little endearing idiosyncrasies of his, dour things they had heard him say; the way he came and went, and didn't give a damn for nobody. Yes he had been a deep old jasper. A real character! And he had belonged to Ridge Pleasant; whenever he wanted a haven in his old age this was it.

Duke listened to the yammering with the cynicism which did not show on his square inscrutable face. But when somebody volunteered they give Zack a real bang-up funeral he said, 'Sure, the old coot had earned it.' But he figured that, wherever he was, the old prospector would be cackling softly over all the shemozzle and the high-faluting talk.

The following morning Duke and Blossom took a light buckboard out of town with them. They travelled to the fringe of the hills, to the scene of last night's tragedy. They had hidden the other three bodies beneath rocks and out of reach of coyotes or buzzards. Now they unearthed them again, placed them on the buckboard and covered them with a blanket. Two of them were Americans, the other a Mexican. Only the contents of the latter's pockets proved interesting, he was carrying a bundle of notes fit to choke a horse.

Although the two men gave the vicinity a thorough going-over they discovered nothing else of any real value. Blossom figured that about half a dozen men had ganged-up on the old man – but why was a mystery.

They lost the tracks of the horses on the hard rock. 'Looks like they've got a hide-out somewhere in the hills,' said Blossom. 'But it's a goldarned maze.'

'They'll certainly be lying low after this,' said Duke, and for the first time since they had found Zack, gave vent to his feelings in a way that made Blossom's blood run cold. If the dry-gulch merchants were caught it would be the rope for them pronto – and no quarter given.

The buckboard was driven back to town and the bodies laid out to view in the undertaking parlour in the hopes that somebody would recognise them and give the law a lead.

Duke, who had another hunch, went over to the bank. He handed the bundle of notes he had taken from the Mexican's pocket over to John Mallibeau and asked him to take a look at them.

'Certainly, Sheriff,' said the banker, handling the greenbacks with loving care.

He placed his pince-nez on his meaty nose and spread the money out on the desk before him. His expression was startled when he looked up. He said:

'Some of this stuff, maybe all of it, came out of the bank.'

That was more than Duke had hoped for. He said: 'How do you know?'

Mallibeau pushed a few of the greenbacks back across the desk. 'Look at that pencilled scribble on them. One of my clerks always uses that when he's checking. Wait, I'll call him....'

The clerk proved to be one of the young shavers who had collected a bop on the noddle during the raid. Although he could not identify the actual notes, they being a mixed batch, he was certainly sure about his own mark.

'Both of you had better come down to the undertaker's and see if you can identify the bozo in whose pocket I found these,' said Duke. Ignoring Mallibeau's anxious look he gathered up the notes and stuffed them into his body-belt.

Neither the manager nor his clerk could identify the dead greaser. Nor it seemed had anybody else so far.

'So he never *drew* this money out of the bank?'

'No sirree,' said the young clerk. 'He's certainly not one of *our* customers.'

'Then he must be one of the bandits,' said John Mallibeau.

'Maybe,' said Duke and would not commit himself further. He promised to return the money to the bank as soon as he had finished with it.

Brock was left with the corpses, to receive the 'viewers' and to report if anything interesting transpired, and Duke joined the other two in the office.

He said: 'Either the three men were members of the stick-up gang or the greaser had the dough from one of them. The first example seems the likeliest....

But why did they stick up Zack? What did a gang like that expect to get out of a broken-down old prospector…?'

'Maybe he'd made a lucky strike,' said Blossom.

'But he was on his way out – surely he hadn't had time….'

Duke paused, his face suddenly grimmer than ever. Then he spoke fast.

'Zack identified the big bearded fellah who I killed the other night as one of a tough-lookin' band he had seen passin' thru' the hills. Isn't it possible that he was gotten out of the way so that he wouldn't be able to identify any more of the band…?'

'But how would they know? They couldn't know that he had identified the man – unless somebody in town told them….'

'That's possible,' said Duke. 'And it would explain a lot of things – including the foolproof slickness of the bank-job. It had obviously been worked out well beforehand….'

'All that is surmise,' said Gil, breaking his own long silence. 'Maybe Zack was killed for robbery after all. Maybe that bunch had broken away from the main band and were doin' some shashaying on their own. Some folks, especially greasers, will murder a man for his boots….'

'But if my surmise is correct that opens up a whole new field of investigation,' said Duke. 'Good job we happened along when we did, even if we were too late to save the ol' man's life.'

Gil, born and bred in this territory, still seemed to pooh-pooh the idea. Nevertheless, the sheriff meant to work on it – though he did not wholly reject the possibility that a newcomer might be the snooper. He decided to investigate all strangers who had lately arrived in the vicinity.

He decided it would serve no useful purpose to go out scouting again right away. If the bandits were lying low in the hills let them think they were safe, maybe they'd get careless. The same applied to the spy in town, if there was such a person, maybe he'd overplay his hand.

The funeral of old Zack was fixed for that afternoon, and at the same time the bodies of the three men who had helped to cause his death would be dropped into an unadorned hole in the ground. Nobody had identified the bodies, they might as well be gotten away before they began to smell. With such cynical speculations the sheriff carried on with his investigations. At the same time his deputies were following his example, as unobtrusively as possible, in other parts of the town.

Duke hit the jackpot first – little knowing what a difference to everything, and himself most of all, his discovery was going to make. It all started in Mother Callaghan's, when he asked the old dame whether she had had any new boarders lately.

She said, in her cracked nasal voice, 'Waal, Sheriff – now you come to remind me – there was a new man came in the day 'fore yestiddy.'

'Why didn't you let me know, Ma?'

'He was such a nice man – a gentleman. A cattle buyer he said he was, come up here to look things over….'

Reflecting that seventy-odd years in the lawless West had evidently not destroyed the old lady's faith in human nature, Duke said:

'Is he here now?'

'Waal no, he ain't here right now. He went out this

mawnin' – said he was going out on the range….'

'He ain't checked out?'

'No, he'd've told me if he wanted to check out. His stuff's still here as far as I know – not that he'd got much…'

'Travelling light, huh?'

Duke was uncertain for a moment. Though Ma erred a little on the tolerant side, her judgement was usually pretty sound. She seemed to have no doubt that her new boarder was a good Joe. Still, there were some bozoes who could smooth-talk people into believing anything – and had a particular line for women. The cattle-dealer line sounded a bit fishy – he hadn't heard of anybody who was doing any selling hereabouts. He decided to go cautiously however, and said to the lady:

'You must understand, Ma, that, with the way things've been happening around here lately, we must check up on all strangers….'

'Yes, Sheriff,' said Ma dutifully.

'All right then, for his sake as well as ours I've got to see into this new boarder of yourn…. When he comes back don't tell him nothin' – just send somebody down to let me know so that I can come an' interview him friendly-like. If he's a nice gent….'

'He is that….'

'All right then, we don't want to scare him none. There's no need to tell him I've been enquiring about him – just let me know he's here…. All right?'

'All right, Sheriff.'

When he got outside Duke heaved a sigh of relief. He'd sooner handle a killer-bronc than a softhearted old woman. When they got an idea into their heads they were just plumb mulish.

He went into the saloon and had a meal, then

joined the rest outside the undertakers in readiness for Zack Mowbray's funeral. The sheriff, together with his three deputies, Frank Heinkel, and the gunsmith, Jamesey Porter, was a bearer. Goatee Matthews was, naturally, chief mourner.

All the townsfolk were there and people rode in from the surrounding ranges. It was quite a jamboree. A real old Western funeral worthy of such a grand old Western character – with the coffin carried on the shoulders of the six bearers as they wended their way slowly up to Boot Hill, and everybody else pacing behind, nobody riding and those of them who brought horses leading them slowly. The old man had always shunned a crowd but he was among one now and he couldn't do a thing about it. Maybe he wouldn't have wanted to anyway – maybe here was the pot of gold that was his final reward; the homage of hard men made suddenly humble; a homage not lightly paid in this pitiless land – and paid only to the true and the great.

The coffin was lowered into the grave on the slopes of Boot Hill where the wind was fresh and clean from the range. Here, beneath the big sky, the old-timer would rest in the wide lands where he had lived and dreamed, and fought and died.

The sky-pilot officiating was an enormously tall and freakishly thin individual known as Hallelluja Charlie. He, appropriately was a dreamer too; a man who asked nothing from life but enough bread to keep body and soul together to praise the Lord over the length and breadth of the West where the folks were sinful and the nights were long. His weapons, the weapons of the Lord he called them, were a Bible, a Frontier Model Colt, a silver tongue, and a pair of bony fists as big as horses' hooves.

The crowd were wrapped in the magic of Charlie's oratory when, looking across the open grave, Duke Pitson saw a man in the crowd opposite watching him. Their eyes seemed to meet for a moment, then the man turned away, tall and as straight as an arrow as he moved through the crowd and vanished from the sheriff's sight. But Duke Pitson, as he lowered his eyes once more to the open grave, and the silvery waves of the preacher's eloquence flowed around him, was troubled by a memory.

When everything was over and the folks began to move back into town a lad came up to the sheriff quietly and told him Mother Callaghan wanted him. Duke gave the boy a coin then moved away fast. When he reached the boarding-house the crowd were behind him and that part of the street was deserted. He slipped up the porch steps and into the soft cool of the lobby. There was a movement in the gloom and his hand went instinctively to his gun. But it was the old lady. She came forward and said:

'He only came in for a moment, Sheriff. Now he's gone out again.'

'I'll wait up in his room for him,' said Duke. 'Give me the key.'

'Sheriff, I hardly like....'

'This is law business, Mrs Callaghan.' His voice was suddenly metallic and he had not called her 'Ma!' She delved into the depths of her voluminous apron and brought forth a bunch of keys. She detached one of them from the rest and handed it over.

'Thank you,' said the sheriff and bowed slightly but with such courtesy that the old lady was a little mollified.

She watched him go up the stairs and shook her head slowly from side to side. Ridge Pleasant was not what it used to be. This last week with all the shooting and murders, the very atmosphere seemed to have changed, and men walked like stalking beasts.

Duke unlocked the door of the room and went inside. He closed the door softly behind him. His glance shuttled around the room, ignoring the commonplace things, seeking something on which to fasten. But there was nothing. It was as if the room was awaiting a tenant instead of already harbouring one. Maybe the man had lit out after all without telling the old lady.

Duke tried to believe that but somehow couldn't. He crossed the room, stooped and looked under the bed. He winced as he went down on his knees and put his hand under there. When he straightened up he held a small pigskin attaché-case in his hand. He placed it on the bed and tried to open it. It was locked. He hesitated for a moment then took out his knife. He unclasped the smallest blade and bent over the case.

It was only a tiny sound he heard but it impinged on his senses like a warning bell. He dropped the knife and whirled, his hand streaking for his gun. But then he let himself go slack, the hand dropping to his side.

A man stood in the now-open doorway and the gun in his hand was pointed right at Duke's chest.

It was the man Duke had seen at Boot Hill, tall, willowy, with a lined thin face and black hair grey-sprinkled beneath his Stetson. A young-old Western man with the cold abysmal eyes of a gun-fighter.

He said: 'Hallo, Bill.'

'Hallo, Milo,' replied the sheriff.

Milo slid a little further into the room and closed the door behind him with his foot. 'Don't try anything, Bill,' he said.

'I'm not completely crazy,' said the sheriff.

Milo said: 'Just to be on the safe side you'd better unbuckle your gunbelt an' let it fall to the floor. Do it gently now – none o' those famous sleight of hand movements of yourn.'

'Not with you, Milo,' said the other as he did as he was told.

There was a little smile on his tight lips but his eyes were blank.

Milo said; 'My, my, two guns now, uh?'

'One of 'em belonged to a friend of mine,' said Duke as he let the weapons fall. 'But you, not having any friends, wouldn't understand that.'

For a moment the other man's cold mask broke; his lips stretched, the killer light flickered unmistakably in the depths of his dark eyes.

Then he was normal again and he said softly, 'I had a friend once – he was killed by a smooth worker who never gave anybody a chance.'

'The only friend you've ever had is your own pride – and it's been your worst enemy too....'

The mask crumpled again and this time the man's teeth showed in a snarl. 'Don't ride me, Bill,' he said thickly, 'or by God I'll kill you right now.'

'I reckon you mean to kill me anyway so what's the use in waiting.'

'I've been waiting a long while – I reckon I can wait a mite longer.'

'Yes – it's been a long time. I admire your tenacity.... But you will learn, Milo, that revenge is not as sweet as it's cracked up to be. I learnt that. If you kill me you will have nothing left to live for.'

'You can forget all your smooth talk. You can't make me change my mind.'

The sheriff smiled again. 'Just the last words of a condemned man.'

For a moment the other smiled with him, saying, 'You allus were a gentlemanly sort of cuss. You fooled a lot of people. You fooled 'em up here too I hear, you an' your sneakin' little pard. Duke and Blossom!' He gave a harsh laugh. 'Fine monikers – the black Duke and his little flower.'

'You like to hear yourself talk don't you?' said Duke.

'I've got plenty of time to talk now. I've had a few years to think out what I'd say to you, what I'd do to you.... I didn't tell you I was still a marshal did I?'

'No, but that makes it easier don't it? You can shoot me down an' call it the law... What might make things awkward though is that I've got lots of friends here – an' I'm a lawman now too you know.' Duke's voice was gently mocking. 'You'd never get away with it; you'd be lynched on the spot. Not a very good ending for your crusade.'

'You clever swine,' said Milo and stepped forward, swinging his gun.

Duke tried to duck but wasn't quite fast enough and the sharp barrel bit into his shoulder. He reeled and the next blow narrowly missed his face. Milo was beside himself with rage. Duke lurched at him, grabbing his body with both hands, trying to pull him down and dodge the gun, all at the same time. Another blow tore a ribbon of flesh from his arm. Milo was like a demon, his madness giving him added strength. A glancing blow at Duke's temple made him reel again in a fire-shot daze. He was sinking.... sinking – and there was a rushing noise and frenzied voices. Then his senses cleared again and he struck out desperately, expecting more blows in return and mightily puzzled when they did not come.

His vision cleared more and he saw Milo squirming on the floor below, and looking up, he found Blossom standing there with a drawn gun.

Duke sat down gingerly on the bed. 'You hurt much?' said Blossom.

Duke felt himself in various places. Then he said: 'Just scratches an' bruises I guess.'

With his hand on the back of his neck, Milo rose to his feet and looked sullenly from one to the other of the two men. Watching him, Blossom's dark face suddenly drained of colour. 'Say the word an' I'll give it to him right now,' he said.

'That wouldn't solve anything,' said Duke.

Milo's lips curled in a sneer. 'Scared?' he said. 'Go on, let him do it an' finish with it – that's what you want....'

'You know I won't,' said Duke. 'Just like you wouldn't when you had me at your mercy. You kept on talking because you knew you couldn't.'

'Horse-feathers,' said Milo. 'I've got a warrant for the arrest of both of yuh an' if you let me free I'll still want yuh – dead or alive.'

Duke smiled again. 'Spoken like a true lawman.'

'Furthermore, if you finish me there'll be others. Now you've been traced they'll keep comin'! You can keep running but they'll keep coming and they'll catch up with you in the end.... There's a price on Bill Prager's head, let him call himself Sheriff Duke Pitson or whatever he likes....'

Blossom and Duke exchanged glances. Milo watched them with a mocking smile. 'You didn't know that did you?' he said.

'No, we didn't,' said Duke. 'You're certainly trying to make your revenge stick aren't you? ... I'm afraid however that you won't make anything stick yet awhile. I've got a job here I mean to finish. An' neither you nor ten like yuh are gonna stop me finishing it if I possibly can....' He leaned forward suddenly. 'Sit down!'

Rather apprehensively the slim man straddled a chair. Duke said: 'You're a gambling man, Milo – the sort of man who'll play out whatever hand's dealt to him.... I'll make a deal with you....'

'I'm always willing to let the other man call,' said Milo. 'What've yuh got?'

EIGHT

Ma Callaghan's old head was in a whirl. Not long after the sheriff went upstairs the man he sought came in and whisked across the lobby as if all the phantoms of the Great Divide were on his heels. When she spoke to him he did not seem to hear her. Presently she was alarmed at hearing a series of ominous bumps from upstairs.

At this juncture the young deputy came in and asked her if the sheriff was here. She did not have time to say anything more but a plain 'Yes' before he too was streaking up the stairs.

After that things became quiet for a bit until she heard footsteps on the stairs and looked apprehensively upwards. The sheriff and his deputy descended towards her, passed her with a brief 'So long, Ma,' and went out into the street. She thought the sheriff looked a bit queer. That was a nasty limp he had. Had he got it when he first came in? She didn't remember.

She suddenly thought about her new boarder and was apprehensive again. Her curiosity got the better of her fear and she began to climb the stairs. She was almost at the top when the boarder himself came into view. 'Mr Platt,' she said, startled.

His face looked very grim, then it softened as he smiled. 'Have yuh got any of that ace-high cawfee of yourn, Ma?' he said.

'Certainly, Mr Platt,' she said. 'I can make some in a jiffy. Come on down into the kitchen.'

'Sure thing,' he said and as she turned he took hold of her arm and they went down together.

Meanwhile Duke and Blossom were entering the *Painted Heifer*. Gil and Brock were already there but the other two lawmen veered away from them and climbed the stairs. They had plenty of curious glances thrown at them. The saloon was packed for, as is the custom with funerals the world over, the mourners, after seeing their friend laid safely to rest, were painstakingly drowning their sorrows.

The two lawman went into Duke's room. The sheriff rolled up his sleeve and scrutinised the long shallow wound made by the sharp sight of Milo's gun. He swabbed it with water from a pitcher on the washstand then taped it up with sticking plaster. It was quite close to the already healing crease he had collected during his gunfight on the street the other night. He had collected more battle-scars in the last few days than in all his life before. He gingerly rubbed a swelling on his head. That would not show beneath his thick red hair anyway.

He opened his shirt and pulled it away from a muscular shoulder. A livid bruise was already beginning to show. He worked his arm around experimentally.

'Stiff,' he said. 'But nothin' to fret about.'

'Matches yuh gammy laig,' said Blossom with a smile. 'Good job you're a two-gun man now.'

'I'll get me a wash an' I'll be all right,' said the sheriff. 'Nothin' about this to anybody, yuh understand?'

'Whadyuh take me for?' said Blossom suddenly nettled. 'It's my pidgeon as well as yours.'

Duke lightly touched the young man's shoulder, and for a moment his cold eyes seemed to soften. It was little more than a gesture and then he was turning away, pouring water into the bowl, reaching soap and towel.

They both slicked themselves up a little. It made them feel better.

As they were leaving the room the door across the hall opened and Dulcie came out.

Duke's face was full in the light as he turned to her and her eyes widened a little. She said:

'Have you been fighting again?'

'No,' said the big man brusquely and he passed on down the passage.

Blossom hesitated. Then he touched his hat and shrugged, and followed.

The girl looked after them and bit her full red underlip. She stood in the passage as if undecided.

Her uncle came out of his room and along to her. He said:

'I've fixed a floor-show for tonight, Pet. It will be on in half-an-hour. Would you like to come down and see it?'

For a moment the girl did not speak.

Finally she said: 'No – o, I don't think so. I have a slight headache. I think I'll stay in my room. May – maybe I'll read a book.' She turned away from him, entered her room, closed the door softly.

Heinkel looked at the blank door and his lean face clouded a little, his shoulders drooped. For a moment all his dandiness seemed to leave him and he looked an old man.

Then he shrugged himself erect, marched on down the stairs.

Duke and Blossom had already reached the bar. Out of the corner of his mouth the latter said:

'You needn't've snubbed the girl.'

'I don't like being fussed,' was the reply. Then Duke was beckoning the barman, and Gil and Brock were joining them as he ordered.

They had a couple of drinks and talked. To the right of them, before the dusty curtains of the small stage, Frank Heinkel was squatting talking to the members of the small four-piece band as they paused in their repertoire.

Suddenly the sheriff raised his hands above his head and shouted: 'Quiet everybody. I've got something to say.'

The talking died a little but there was still a burbling undertone. With a flick of his wrist Duke drew one of his guns, elevated it, pressed the trigger. The heavy Colt boomed, making the glasses rattle, bringing a miniature shower of dust from the ceiling.

Frank Heinkel shot erect, his eyes widening a little. Then they became smoky once more, watching the sheriff.

The room was still. Everybody was still now. Everybody looked at Duke as he slowly holstered his gun. His face was as expressionless as ever.

'Hope I didn't scare anybody,' he said. 'Whoever was scared 'ud better drop out before I start talkin'. What I've got to say won't interest them anyway.... I want as many good men as I can get to form a posse an' ride with me up into the hills pronto. It may be an all-night job 'cos we've got to comb those hills like we were lookin' for dogies in a prickly patch. An' it might be a dangerous job 'cos we may run into what we're lookin' for – the gang who robbed the bank – the gang maybe who killed ol' Zack Mowbray. If we do find 'em, and as that is what we'll be going out there for, I certainly hope we do, we're gonna have a helluva battle on our hands. I want you all to know what you may be up against. You might get a slug in the guts, and on the other hand, all you might get is sore feet. It's all in the cards. That's all I've got to say.'

People began to move forward. That was all he'd got to say! But it was plenty for such a taciturn cuss as Duke. Then everybody began to talk at once as they flocked forward to be with him.

Frank Heinkel pushed his way through the mob. Men stood aside to let him pass. He was a big one in this man's town. Bigger even than the new sheriff – socially if not in size. He reached Duke's side and hissed:

'I'd got a show all fixed up to go on in a few minutes.'

'I'm sorry, Frank,' said Duke out of the corner of his mouth.

A little smile flickered across the saloon owner's face. 'All right,' he said. 'I'll cancel the show and I'll come along with you and get me a bandit's scalp – maybe.'

'You're welcome,' said Duke.

It was a small army that swept down the main drag half-an-hour later and out on to the trail. The night was very dark, each man could see only his immediate neighbour. The air was oppressive, threatening rough weather.

In the forefront rode Duke, Blossom, Gil, Brock and Heinkel. Behind them the mob was jubilant and talkative until the galloping hooves brought them near the hills. Then their silence became pronounced, and menacing by contrast.

As the ground began to slope upwards to the foothills the sheriff urged his mount forward and turned him. Then he stood up in his stirrups and held his hands aloft.

The band drew to a halt, horses' hooves scrabbling on the hard ground, the clink of harness and the creak of saddle leather. A curse here and there as a man chided a restive beast and then murmured softly to quieten him. Then silence fell like a blanket over the dark mass that was a mob of horsemen beneath the lowering sky. And, even the horses were suddenly very quiet as if in understanding.

All that could be heard was the faint sound of a wind that was like a sulphurous breath from hell. Then the sheriff spoke. He did not raise his voice but it was clear and the words carried.

'We'll split up into three parties and spread out. I'll take one. Blossom and Gil can take the other. And Brock and Frank can take the third. We'll start off separately. Brock – Frank, you pick your men and break off to the left.'

'All right,' said Brock.

Heinkel rode forward and spoke quietly to the sheriff.

'I'm not so used to this kind of game as some of the old-timers here. I wouldn't want to insult them by attempting to lead them. I'll stick with you.'

Duke was a little nonplussed by his ex-boss's suddenly diffident manner. But he shrugged and said:

'Suit yourself, Frank.'

He kneed his horse past the saloon-owner and found Brock in the dark. Visibility was mighty poor and that made things difficult. Nevertheless, by this time the band had gotten itself sorted out into three roughly proportionate sections.

After Brock had had a little palaver with his boss he led his band away.

Duke raised his voice again. 'The alarm signal will be three shots!'

Blossom and Gil led their men off to the right. Duke saw them away then, with Heinkel at his side, led his own section forward in a straight line, making for the highest point of the hills, the towering lump of rock and sandstone known as the Sugar Loaf.

As he rode the ex-gambler remembered what Goatee, the old storekeeper had told him about old Zack being bound for there. Goatee had been mighty reluctant to divulge the fact too. Maybe the old prospector had gotten on to something good after all. Maybe those bushwhackers *had* been after something – a map, a letter...? That certainly would mean a new deal....

Aw, no.... he was letting his fancies run away with him; Zack had never panned anything but enough dust to get the necessities for him and his beloved beasts. Though the hand *was* dealt that way sometimes; a man hit the jackpot and it blew right up in his face! Maybe Zack had found a bonanza and because he was made to be poor, had always been happy poor, the deity ordained he should die as he had lived, and that men, instead of envying him, should honour him....

Pretty soon Duke had to quit speculating and concentrate on guiding and gentling his horse as the climb became steep and tortuous. Finally the horses were scrambling and snorting and making more noise than was comfortable in what was likely to be enemy territory. They settled down a bit when the party reached a shelf of flat ground; a freak deposit on the side of the craggy slopes, which even had stunted trees sprouting from them.

Duke decided the safest plan would be to leave the horses there. This was done and the men proceeded, more silently, on foot.

The night was even blacker among these rocks. Men plunged suddenly into abysmal clefts and gullies, and were groping alone. Men turning to whisper to an immediate neighbour, discovered he was not there any more.

Heinkel was a silent wraith moving to the right of Duke. Scrabbling sounds to the left denoted that somebody else was quite near but Duke could not see the man. It would be a ticklish business if they did suddenly run into somebody. For a moment the sheriff wished he had not been so durned anxious to get to grips with something.

One consolation was that *they* could not be seen either. But that gink on the left! he was making so much noise he might as well be banging a big drum.

'Take it easy,' hissed the sheriff. 'D'yuh want to awaken all the folks back in Ridge Pleasant?'

'Sorry, Duke,' said the plaintive voice. 'It's these goldarned new boots o' mine.'

The man came closer, keeping pace with him, and looking the other way, Duke realised he had lost Heinkel. There were sounds all around, little scratching, rustling sounds like those made by a colony of mice.

Then the very rocks around seemed to explode as three shots rang out. The alarm! Fired from somewhere ahead of the party.

Duke and his shadowy companion froze in their

tracks. The sheriff's brain was racing. Who had fired the alarm, and why? Had they suddenly stumbled on the people they sought? He had seen no flashes. The shots might almost have been fired in the depths of the earth – the echoes rolling away up in the hills.

Then he heard movements up ahead. Somebody was being too hasty!

Even as he screamed, 'Down!' and flung himself on his belly, the night disintegrated once more. There were flashes now, plenty of them, and the gunfire rolled like thunder. Bullets hissed, smacking into the rocks, or whining like angry hornets as they ricocheted.

Duke realised he was lying on the edge of a cleft very like that one in which Zack Mowbray had been found. These slopes were durned treacherous. But he could not give much thought to terrain as he elevated his gun and fired back at the flashes. He could sense his own men all around him and was deafened by gunfire as they opened up. He wondered which of them it was who had given the alarm. He had seemed to be in front too; a smart gink whoever he was – the whole bunch of them would have walked into an ambush if those three shots had not been fired. He wondered if the other two parties had heard them and were beginning to move this way.

His thoughts were a little jumbled but his brain was ice-cold, his trigger-fingers steady on his two guns, his thumbs slamming the hammers. He was firing blind for, even in the flashes, men could not be distinguished from distorted rock-shapes. He fired at tongues of flame, hoping to hit the men behind them. He realised he was almost alone. His left-hand neighbour had either been hit or had moved over to better cover. Frank Heinkel had vanished as if the earth had swallowed him. Was it he who had fired the shots…?

Above the din he heard a shrill rising scream and wondered whether it was one of *his* slugs that had found a target. He could sense the presence of men moving up around him. There was one suddenly at his elbow and he half-turned. The shape seemed to move faster then. Something exploded on his head with blinding force and he began to fall. Over the edge of the cleft into blackness…. falling…. falling….

NINE

The ambushers were in cover at the base of the Sugar Loaf itself and as the attackers advanced they began to move away around the back of it.

As the firing died for a moment somebody shouted in the distance. One of the sheriff's men answered the hail while the others wondered why they did not hear their leader's voice. Had he stopped one?

It seemed that one, or both, of the two other parties were moving up. And it was evident that the ambushers, judging by their spasmodic shooting and the range of it, were retreating.

'After 'em!' yelled somebody, and impelled by that voice, the attackers threw caution to the wind and began to charge ruggedly over the tortuous ground.

The other band's fire was scattered and did little harm. It was further away than ever. There was less of it.

Suddenly the attackers found themselves up against the base of the Sugar Loaf. And there was nothing and nobody there. They quit firing, fearful of hitting one of their own side, jostling a little, awaiting a lead.

Then from the other side of the Sugar Loaf, mocking as the echoes bounced from the rock walls, whispered among the sandstone, came the clatter of horses' hooves.

'Goddam it!' yelled somebody. 'They'd got critturs stashed away out back there.'

Men began to move around the sides of the Sugar Loaf. Back there the landscape opened up a little, going downwards. Men began to blaze away, cursing in frustration, knowing that they probably would not hit anything, knowing they could not follow on foot. Although it had not been possible for them to bring their own mounts up the perilous way they had followed, the ambushers had evidently not had the same difficulty. It was obvious that they knew these hills hellishly well.

A voice shouted again from way back, but nearer this time. One of the sheriff's men answered and pretty soon the other band came up. They were led by Gil and Blossom.

'Duke!' cried the latter.

Nobody answered him. 'Where's Duke?' he said, there was a note of alarm in his voice.

Men began to talk to their nearest neighbours or to members of the other band, vague shapes with voices in the stillness. At this juncture Brock and his gang moved in. The situation was explained to them by sundry voices and there was much useless cursing. Their quarry had gotten clean away and it looked like they had lost their leader.

The voice of Frank Heinkel suddenly rang out. 'Duke was near me until just before the shooting started…. I didn't see him afterwards. There was too much going on. I don't know what happened to him.... I guess some of our men weren't so lucky as the rest of us. Maybe Duke....'

'Show some lights and start lookin,' interrupted Blossom harshly.

Matches were struck, the flames blossoming like glow-worms in the darkness. Everybody had given up hope of catching the ambushers. They were apprehensive now, each one beginning to realise that, even if *he* had escaped unscathed, others may not have done so. Men looked for relatives; for friends; for the sheriff, their well-liked leader.

There was a sharp exclamation from one man as he bent over something among the rocks, the flame dying in his hand as if to symbolise the still thing its holder had found. Blossom was swiftly beside the man. They both struck matches and Blossom went down on his knees beside the still form.

He let out a breath of relief. 'It's not one of our men,' he said.

'That's one who didn't get away,' said the other man and their flames died in their fingers. But all around others were blossoming, making the darkness velvety. The wind was dying and the little flames shot upwards. The air was heavier.

They continued to search in ever-widening circles and they found another body. It was that of Bruff Larue, a gin-sodden loafer of Ridge Pleasant. A no-good he had been, but one who could never resist a fight. Maybe he would have wished to die that way.

A little group of men were standing around the body when the first heavy drops of rain plummeted from the sky. Then the clouds split apart with a ragged tongue of flame and the thunder rattled as if another attack was beginning.

The rain came in a blinding, buffeting sheet. Flames were snuffed and men groped in pitch blackness. It was an ironic culmination to a night of failure and tragedy.

Slowly, in scattered bunches, dripping and cursing while nature unleashed its fury upon their heads, they made their way down to their horses.

Luckily the beasts had been tethered. Men found them and gentled them with hands and voices as they milled, and the lightning lit the scene in a garish pantomime.

They sheltered among stunted trees or huddled beneath overhanging lips of rock and gradually the skies began to lighten, the downpour to lose some of its violence. But it still came down with steady monotony and the sage old-timers of the company voiced the opinion that it was set in for the night.

Blossom led a band away and they searched again for Duke but with no success. They had no light and the going was hard and perilous. The climax came when one man fell and broke his ankle and had to be carried moaning back to his horse. Then even the faithful deputy had to admit that it was useless to look further for his friend tonight.

Sick at heart he returned to the assembled company and gave the word to ride. They moved off in the rain, a sorry, silent company bound homewards with news of an abject failure. And very many of them were heavy-hearted at the thought that they would never see straight shooting Duke Pitson alive again.

Blossom had not given up hope. Duke could not be dead – he was immortal and a leader of men; it was not in the cards that he should die yet – it couldn't be! But what could he do? – with the night still so black and the rain coming down with unceasing monotony. The sense of his own helplessness brought blinding frustration which almost quelled his hope…. But a flame of it still flickered. Duke and he had been friends and partners for so long, like brothers they had been; wouldn't he know if the big man was dead? Wouldn't something inside of him tell him so? Maybe Duke was tracking those bushwhackers….

In the minds of the rest of them there was little doubt that the sheriff was dead, lying back there among the rocks in the rain with the body of one of his enemies. Their regret was that they had not found him – to bring him home as they were bringing the no-good Bruff Larue…. But already Blossom had decided to go back at dawn which was not far away. He told Gil and Brock of his resolution and they elected to go along with him.

When the wretched cavalcade rode into Ridge Pleasant the folks awakened to receive them. Frank Heinkel gave orders for the *Painted Heifer* to be opened and a bunch of 'the girls' helped, for a change, by the matrons of the town set to brewing coffee and lacing it with rum.

The news of the loss of Duke Pitson passed from mouth to mouth. He had been a straight shooter, and the women averred, a gentleman in every sense of the word. Dulcie came downstairs to see to a few of the men who had flesh wounds. The news was thrown at her, chocker-block, by a buxom matron.

'Duke Pitson got kilt. They cain't find his body.'

Blossom had his eyes on Dulcie as the loud-mouthed woman spoke. He saw the colour fade from the girl's face, leaving it an ashen mask with staring eyes. He ran to her side and put his arm around her shoulders as she swayed.

'We don't know, Dulcie,' he said. 'Nobody saw it happen. Take no notice of these blabber-mouths. I know he isn't dead. I'm going out after him as soon as it's light…'

In his heart he prayed fervently that the things he said were true as he felt the girl's slim body shaking and knew she was fighting to control herself, not to reveal her feelings to the gossips around. He realised then the truth of what he had suspected since the very day that Dulcie had come home. Duke couldn't be dead. *He couldn't!* Not with this lovely girl waiting for him.

He nodded his head at Dulcie's whisper. Then she said:

'I'll be all right now, Blossom, thank you.'

He left her then and when he returned to look at her again she was expertly bandaging an old-timer's scrawny arm. Her face was pale and set but no more so than many of the womenfolk there. He admired the guts of the kid. She was grand old Western stock and not unused to violence and sorrow.

The bare essence of her story flashed through his mind as, after gulping a hot drink he ran upstairs to change into dry clothes.

When she was six years old her father, Frank Heinkel's brother, and her mother had been killed in a cattle-stampede. It had been just such a night as this that it had happened too. The beasts had been maddened by thunder and lightning, and every available hand on the small ranch had been mustered to attempt to avert a disaster that would mean ruin. With the ranch owner came his wife, a lusty young frontierswoman. They died together.

What cattle that could be caught and everything that remained on the ranch was sold to pay off debts, and Dulcie, the only daughter was handed over to the guardianship of her only traceable kin, Frank Heinkel, who at that time ran a little honky-tonk gambling-house, in Phoenix. He was a taciturn man who had little truck with womenfolk, except those of the lowest kind, whom he hired to entertain his guests and treated like chattels. Into this bawdy though colourful life, the little girl from the quiet windswept range was roughly pitchforked. At first she was scared of her uncle Frank and the people he had gathered around him.

But the gambling-house keeper was kind to her in his silent rather forbidding way and she was soon intrigued by shuffling cards, the balls flashing and clicking in the wheels, the brassy-voiced women who sang and danced, the occasional shooting. Pretty soon her memory of the life before she arrived there was very vague, a soft dream that came on her at times and made her young heart a little sad.

Her uncle did not like her to enter the honky-tonk and gambling house but oft-times she got lonely in her little room and crept along the landing to the top of the stairs and stood, hidden in the shadows, watching the panorama below. The scene was laid out before her beneath the glow of the arc-lamps. Ever shifting – ever colourful. She saw many things. Drunkenness; joy; the sadness of a man watching his last cent go into the coffers of the dealer; fights; shooting; a man killed, the blood welling in a fascinating crimson stream from a head spotlighted garishly by the lamps.

Once there was a big fight and a man ran upstairs towards Dulcie, and with his back to her, threatened the room with two guns. Her uncle walked slowly up towards him, talking all the time, and the man said, 'All right, Frank,' and descended with him. Dulcie knew that her uncle was very brave. She knew, too, that he had seen her standing there as, his arm around the other man's shoulders, he had looked back up the stairs.

That night he beat her. It was the only time he had ever beat her and she would never forget it.

Although Frank Heinkel did not always understand her he was very good to her. When she got older he told her more about her parents and their struggle for existence in the pitiless Western lands. He would never struggle as they had done, he had other ways, but he promised her that some day when he had enough money he would buy a big ranch and she would be its mistress.

When Frank Heinkel moved to Ridge Pleasant it was a cluster of shacks and tents without a name. He helped to put it on the map; built its biggest saloon. And, with money rolling in, the promised ranch seemed much nearer. But the bawdy life of the saloon, the honky-tonk, the gambling-house, although he kept always a little aloof from its rougher elements, seemed to hold a fascination for Heinkel. He coined money and he kept on coining it. He sent Dulcie to school back East and promised her that when she came back, a grown-up educated young lady, they would do some more about having the finest ranch in the whole West.

Yes, Blossom knew the story well, many times he and Duke had heard it from Dulcie's lips as she dangled her legs from a fence or squatted on the top of the back stoop. The ranch – that was her dream; and he and Duke had seemed almost part of it. Maybe Blossom had had a dream too in those far off days. A dream of a brown-skinned girl who would grow up side by side with him and never leave him. Such dreams were not for such as he so he let it fade and only recalled it from time to time with a faint nostalgia. Now it was irrevocably dead. Another dream had taken its place – another person's dream which he had to make come true. To bring the only two people he had ever loved in this world together again – although he was not sure that one of them could ever be brought back any more.

He finished changing himself and went downstairs and got his horse ready. He awaited the dawn.

At the end of the street the sky began to lighten and turn to a pearly grey. The rain had stopped and there was a soft glow in the early morning air. Everything promised a fine day.

The smoky-eyed young man with the lean drawn face noticed these signs automatically. He had seen many dawns, in all kinds of circumstances, but never in one so forlorn as now. Gil and Brock came out to him and mounted their horses. The three of them rode side by side, and as they thundered out on the trail, there was a pink smoky haze in the morning sky.

Duke Pitson's ascension from out of the black pit into which he had fallen was slow and painful. First of all was a weak groping in an atmosphere that was like black clinging wool. And even when this was pulled away by his clawing hands it only revealed another layer of milky greyness. He realised he was lying on his back and his movements had not been physical but only in his mind.

He began to move then, tentatively, as memory came back to him. He came to the conclusion that, though he was stiff and bruised there were no bones broken. The haziness had been caused by his head, which now felt big as two, and was screaming with pain. He raised his hand and ran his fingers lightly along his face, feeling the dried blood and upwards to where it was caked on a painful swelling. Then full memory returned with a rush.

He had been hit over the head with something – probably a gun-butt – by somebody who had leapt at him from the darkness. He had not expected any of the ambushers to be that near, and was skittled like a sitting duck. He was lucky the man had not pumped a slug into him. The ambusher had doubtless been chary of giving his position away.

Duke remembered the sensation of falling. Now he realised that sensation had been no trick of his mind. He had tumbled into the rock-cleft at the edge of which he had been lying.

Rock walls were very close each side of him. The cleft was about six feet deep and that strip of grey above him was the sky.

He put his hands on the rocks each side and began to lever himself upwards. His wounded head screamed in protest and a groan was forced from his lips. Then he was upright, sweat beading his forehead as he leaned weakly against the rock face.

Gradually the tumult died. He stood on tiptoe and looked over the edge of the cleft. The terrain was desolate and craggy. To the right of him rose the Sugar Loaf. A ground mist crept over the ground and lingered in the hollows, giving everything an eerie appearance.

Dawn was breaking.

Duke Pitson hauled himself up and for a moment squatted on all fours at the edge of the cleft. When he had fallen in there it had been night. He had been there quite a time. The stiffness and coldness of his body testified to that fact; the feeling was not wholly caused by bruises. He realised he must have lain there unseen and had probably been given up for dead. He wondered what had happened to the rest of the men.

The mist was damp and clung to him. The rocks were wet beneath him as if there had been a storm. It was as if he had been dropped into another world. Every new discovery gave him childish pleasure. He felt his clothes. They were stiff and wet, drying on him. No wonder he was stiff and cold.

He crawled across to a nearby boulder. There was a patch of dry sand beneath it. He turned over and squatted on his haunches with his back against the cold rock. Every movement sent stabs of needle-like pain through his wounded head. But his senses were becoming much clearer.... It'd take more than a crack on the noddle to get *him* down.

He reached in his hip-pocket and got his little sack of 'makings'. The sack, tied tightly at the mouth, was made of wash leather. He was overjoyed when he discovered that the contents were dry. He took out a paper, a large pinch of baccy, and rolled himself a quirly. There were matches there too, in a small flat box. He struck one and lit up. He took a few deep drags and was mightily soothed. Then he smoked slowly and ruminated.

The mist was clearing around him. The sky was lightening and taking on a pinky tinge.

Duke's eyes, slowly raking the territory within range, suddenly lighted on a dark bundle; no rock or vegetation.

He rose to his feet, stood erect for a while until his head ceased to spin, then walked across to the object.

It was a dead man all right. Duke was mightily relieved to discover it was nobody he knew.

The man had been shot in the side of the head. He looked like a half-breed. Duke went down on one knee beside him and began to go through his pockets. He found nothing of value. A sack of 'makings' very like his own; a wicked-looking clasp knife; a few coins and a small roll of notes; a crucifix. Pitiful things.

The man's shirt and embroidered vest were ragged, his leather chaps well-worn. In contrast his gunbelt was new and of fancy Mexican style, broad, thick, chased and studded in silver. The holster was of tooled leather, slightly greased, and working on a swivel so that, at a touch of the hand, it dropped to an easy position for a quick draw.

The man's gun lay close to his hand. It was a heavy forty-eight with a silver-studded mother-of-pearl butt. It was well-oiled, and consequently the rain had done it little harm.

Duke spun the chambers and extracted the remaining four damp shells. He rolled the body flat on its back and extracted all the dry shells he could find from the cartridge-belt. He reloaded the gun and put the rest of the ammunition in his back pocket. While he was about it he examined the ammunition in his own gunbelt. Most of it was useless. The few shells that were any good he put with the others.

Now he had three guns all told. Although they had all been exposed to the rain surely at least one had adequate firing properties. He might need it too, being in enemy territory and not having any idea of how things had finished up last night.

TEN

He was standing, debating with himself on what course to pursue, when he heard the hoofbeats, echoing from behind the bulk of the Sugar Loaf. He looked around him quickly then limped a few yards and squatted behind a huge boulder.

The hoofbeats came nearer then stopped. He heard the horses pawing the rock and knew they had been left. Then two men came around the corner of the Sugar Loaf.

One was a Mexican; the other a big American, a palpable ex-cowhand. They were a villainous looking pair.

'Here he is,' said the big man and pointed to the body.

'Let us get heem then and get away from here in case those people are still around,' said the Mexican.

'I can't understand why Mancey wanted to send us all the way back here for a stiff 'un,' grumbled the big man.

'Mancey ees clever,' said the other. 'He wasn't sure Jacko was dead. Mebbe he was still alive and could talk. Then again, if he was dead, mebbe he could be identified. You know Mancey does not like any of us to be identified.'

'Yeh, I guess he knows what he's doin'.'

They stopped by the body. 'You take his laigs, I'll take his shoulders,' said the big man and they both bent to the task.

Duke waited till they had lifted the body and were stumbling away with it over the craggy ground then he came out from cover and barked:

'All right, amigos. Stay right where you are. Don't drop the man.'

The Mexican's eyes flared and he let go of one of the legs he held. Then he had a good look at the big menacing figure with the two guns and lifted the limb again, clinging to it for dear life. The big man, his back bowed a little with the weight of the dead man's head and shoulders, stood rigid.

Duke strode forward. He holstered one of his own guns then swiftly lifted those of the two men, together with a nasty-looking little toothpick the greaser had tucked into his dirty silk sash. With a swing of his arm he flung these weapons as far away as he could.

'You can drop Joe now, amigos,' he said. 'Then elevate yuh paws.'

'Joe' fell with a dull thud and rolled over on his face. Two pairs of hands reached for the clouds. Duke worked his way around behind them. Now he had a couple of captives, dropped to him out of the skies so to speak, he was not quite sure what to do with them.

They didn't appear to be very courageous speci-mens. Maybe if he knocked them around a little one of them would talk. He moved nearer....

It was only a tiny sound behind him. It impinged

on his senses rather than on his ears. He whirled, firing from the hip. The man who had come around the corner of the Sugar Loaf and was taking aim for a nice finishing shot in the back was taken by surprise. He clutched at his side with his free hand, his eyes bulging, his mouth open wide. He tried to bring his gun level.

Duke fired again, saw him begin to topple, then turned to meet the onslaught of the other two men. His gun was torn from his hand by the clawing fingers of the Mexican. Duke swung out with his fist, felt it jar on bone. Then the big man was upon him, an iron-hard arm was clamping around his throat, choking him as his head was forced back. The Mexican danced around in front of him, raising his fists, beating them again and again into Duke's face. Each blow sent pain down through his wounded head, like the sharp point of a pick-axe, driving deep. Then everything went numb and he had that sensation of falling once more.

He did not fall all the way this time; he seemed to be suspended in a haze. He had a vague feeling of being carried, then dumped. Then there was a jolting, swaying sensation that, with full returning consciousness, became pain and smell. The pain of his throbbing head and bleeding face, the pungent stink of horseflesh in his nostrils.

He was sagged forward against a horse's mane and his ankles were tied beneath its belly. His hands were tied too – behind his back. He let his head roll. His eyes were half-open and he could see the Mexican and the big man riding each side of him.

His head was bare and he could feel the morning sunlight warm on his neck. The ground was flatter and smoother beneath the horse's hooves. They began to thud into shifting sand and he realised they were somewhere in the badlands that began just behind the Sugar Loaf. He was puzzled. Surely the men did not mean to take him right across that wide stretch of treacherous country? No, maybe they had a more sinister purpose in mind.

Trying to think only made his head worse. He let everything ride for a bit and closed his eyes once more, letting his head sink into the horse's mane. There was something very comforting about the warmth of the animal, the familiar smell.

Swinging along with the rhythm of the horse's movements he fell into a half doze. How long it lasted he did not know but he was jolted out of it by an elbow thrust suddenly, violently into his ribs.

'Quit playin' possum, Sheriff,' said the voice of the big man. 'Look alive. You're nearly at the end o' the trail. Sit up, damn you!' A hand grabbed his shoulder and pulled him erect in the saddle.

Duke turned and looked at the man. 'You know who I am?' he said.

'I know who you are all right. You killed one o' my pards in Ridge Pleasant the other night.'

'Take a good look at me,' said Duke. 'I'm goin' to kill you too.'

The man let out an oath and swung his fist. Duke swayed back in the saddle, causing the blow to miss its mark. The big fellah was poising himself for another try when the Mexican said:

'I should quit that, amigo. Mancey 'ull want him to be talking when he sees him.'

'Yeh, mebbe you're right,' said the big man. 'Mebbe Mancey'll let me work him over later. Mebbe if he won't talk....'

Presently, from out of the arid, cactus-dotted plain

before them, a mirage seemed to rise; a cluster of buildings with a crumbling hacienda in the centre. The ghost-town of Sundown. At first Duke Pitson thought it was indeed a mirage but as, with each jog of his horse, it became clearer, he realised what it must be.

He had heard about Sundown but this was the first time he had seen it. He remembered the garbled tales he had been told about it. It was a fitting place to leave a dead body. His mind shied away from that thought and he remembered instead the man he had shot back there in the hills. For the first time he looked behind him. He could hardly suppress a shudder at what he saw.

The men had brought the body along with them. It was being dragged at the end of a rope which was tied to the pommel of the Mexican's saddle. It bumped and spun along, raising a small cloud of sand.

Duke's brain was working fast now. There should be two bodies. They must have buried the other one. What kind of a game were they playing? He remembered their talk, their mention of a man called Mancey; the boss no doubt! Who was Mancey, and where did he hang out?

Over the border probably. And this ghost-town was the halfway post of his men's journey. Maybe they had food and drink stashed here.... He did not expect to see anyone else in Sundown and consequently was mightily surprised when a man came walking towards them with a carbine in the crook of his arm.

He waved as they passed him and Duke looked back to see him following them leisurely in.

They halted for a moment and the Mexican cut

the body free and left it lying in the dust behind them. Looking back as they moved on Duke saw two men come out of one of the hovels and bend over the body. Then the small cavalcade halted again outside the ruined hacienda.

The Mexican slid from his horse and cut the ropes that bound Duke's ankles. The sheriff tried to kick out at him. But his limbs were too numb, he was slow and missed his mark. The Mexican grinned and drove a fist into the pit of his stomach. He fell from his horse and rolled.

They dragged him to his feet and urged him through a small door in the hacienda wall. A man met them with a gun, said 'Howdy,' staring curiously at Duke as they passed him.

The Mex knocked at the door around the bend of the stone passage and a voice said: 'Come in.'

The Mex opened the door. The big man buffeted Duke in the back, sending him staggering into the room.

'Got a present f're yuh, Mancey,' he said. 'The sheriff of Ridge Pleasant.'

Duke found himself looking at a thin man who stood erect behind a desk. He had a very narrow yellow face that was slashed in half by a thick black moustache. His eyes were small and narrow, and black. He reminded the big man of a diamond-backed rattlesnake.

The lips curled a little beneath the moustache but the eyes remained glassy and evil.

The man said: 'This is an unexpected honour, Sheriff Pitson. Welcome to our humble abode.'

It was past noon when the three deputies rode back into Ridge Pleasant. They hitched their horses outside the *Painted Heifer* and went inside. Men followed them down the street and into the saloon, joining the motley that was already in there. The men leaned against the bar, their eyes red-rimmed from looking into the sun, their clothes filthy with dust, and sipped liquor through cracked lips. Then they told their story.

One of the barmen said to Blossom: 'The boss told me to tell yuh he'd like to see yuh as soon as you came in. He seems almighty worried about Duke.'

'All right, I'll go up,' said Blossom.

He mounted the stairs slowly, turned along the landing. Frank Heinkel came out of his room at the end. They met in the middle of the passage. Heinkel did not speak. The expression of his lined face was interrogative.

Blossom said: 'We can't find any trace of him. But I'm not giving up.'

Heinkel said: 'It looks like the bushwhackers took the body with them.'

A door opened behind him and he turned. Dulcie stood there, her face washed of all colour, her eyes dark and enormous.

Blossom said quickly: 'There's still hope, Miss Dulcie. I haven't given up.'

She said dully: 'I heard what Uncle said.'

Heinkel said: 'I was silly, my dear. Jumping to conclusions. Blossom is right. We mustn't give up hope.'

The girl did not say any more but backed into her room and closed the door. The two men exchanged glances. 'I'll get moving,' said Blossom and turned on his heels.

Frank Heinkel turned too, in the opposite direction, and knocked on Dulcie's door. There was no reply so he opened it.

The girl was sitting on her bed with her hands lying in her lap. She was staring at the opposite wall but she looked at her uncle as he came into the room and closed the door behind him.

Her look was blank. In the light from the window her face looked strained.

He sat on the bed beside her, touching her shoulder tentatively with his hand.

With a convulsive movement she turned and fell forward on his breast. Sobs began to shake her body.

Through them her voice whispered. 'I loved him, uncle, I loved him,' and the man stroked her hair and looked past it with tortured eyes into a hell of his own creating, his own schemes crumbling in dust and ashes around him.

After a little while she straightened up and said, 'I'm all right now, uncle.'

She rose, crossed to a chair by the window and sat down. She looked out of the window. Heinkel sat on the bed, his head downcast.

'I've been thinking of negotiating for a site just outside Tucson and building that big ranch we always said we'd have. I wanted to talk to you about it first…. What do you think? It's time we moved away from this place. Tucson's up-and-coming. There's more for a young educated lady to do up there….'

'Yes uncle, that would be fine,' she said.

Her voice was listless. Heinkel rose. 'Don't give up hope, my dear,' he said. 'We cannot know Duke is dead until we find his body. Dead men don't walk. He must have done so or he would have been found by now.'

The girl did not answer. Her head was averted now. She was looking through the window. Heinkel crossed the room and stood beside her looking down into the street. He could hardly suppress a start at something he saw out there.

Dulcie seemed hardly aware of him now. She did not turn as he left her side, left the room, closing the door softly behind him. His shoulders were bowed, he looked suddenly old as he went along the passage and entered his own room once more.

It was two rooms actually, a sitting-room and a smaller bedroom. He crossed to the door of the latter, opened it and passed through. Beside his bed was another door, covered by a red curtain and always kept locked and bolted.

He swung aside the curtain, turned the key in the lock, reached up and slid the bolt. He opened the door. A man was coming up the back stairs towards him.

He was a Mexican in very showy clothes, which, though well-worn, gleamed with silver and pearl. His sombrero was high-crowned and had tassels around the edges of its abnormally wide brim.

Heinkel held the door open, and as the man came nearer, hissed, 'Juan, I told you never to come here.'

With a catlike movement the Mexican slid past him into the room. He said:

'Mancey said it was ver' important. He'd like to see yuh as soon as you can make it. I've been hanging around outside trying to see yuh….'

'Yes, I know, I saw you; lounging about in full view of everybody. Dressed up like a Xmas tree. And at just the time when all the townsfolk are mighty suspicious of strangers. I saw one of the sheriff's deputies displaying a more than ordinary interest in you.'

'Nobody knows me here,' said Juan. 'I wasn't in on the bank robbery. And I come from the other side of the border.'

'People will begin to wonder if they saw you come up my backstairs....'

'Nobody saw me. I made sure of that.'

'What's eating Mancey?'

'He didn't say. He just told me to ask you to come if you could manage it.'

'All right,' said Heinkel. 'Get going. Be careful.'

'Adios,' said Juan and went. Heinkel locked and bolted the door immediately behind him then went hurriedly into his sitting-room.

Blossom was coming out of the saloon when he saw the Mexican on the other side of the street. Juan was a bird of bright plumage and little wits who dearly loved to preen himself before the public eye. He was a stranger and a very noticeable one, and as Heinkel had feared, Blossom was mighty curious.

On an impulse he crossed the road leisurely, thankful that his deputy's star was in his vest pocket instead of displayed prominently on his chest. Behind the Mexican, lounging against the hitching-rack was a small store kept by a half-breed called Jimmy Bang. Blossom passed quite close to the man and left the sun-glare of the street for the dusky interior of the shop.

Jimmy came out from the dim recesses in the back, his round oily face beaming like a beacon.

Blossom said softly: 'Do you know that man outside?'

Jimmy peered, squinting with his little eyes. Then he shook his head.

'How long has he been there?'

Jimmy shook his head again 'I hadn't noticed him before.'

Blossom said, 'Gimme a sack o' baccy.' Then, as

the half-breed went back behind his counter, he moved nearer to the window and looked out. He knew that the Mexican, even if he turned his head, would not be able to see into the gloom of the shop whereas he, full in the glare of the sunlight, was a perfect picture. Blossom studied him at his leisure. He was leaning nonchalantly against a hitching post. An admirable side-view!

The man's apparel was certainly a sight for sore eyes. The pipe-stem trousers with conchoes and charms stitched all down the seams. The trousers, the better to display their magnificence, were worn over the high-heeled riding-boots which made them bulge in danger of splitting at the calves. At the heels of the boots were spiked silver rowels, over large, and cruel to any beast. Why did most 'greasers' favour them? Was it for display only? The black velvet sombrero with tassels around the wide brim. The embroidered vest, also sewn with silver charms. The low-slung gun in its ornamental holster. The silk purple sash....

Blossom moved closer to the window for a better look. There was something about the man's appearance that struck a chord in his mind. It was those silver ornaments – winking and shining in the sunlight.

He remembered suddenly the silver charm he had found near the garrotted man, dead beneath the pitiless desert sun.

The shape of some of the things on that man's apparel, on his vest particularly, were very like, if not identical to that charm. Was not there some way he could get a closer look...?

Jimmy came over to him with the sack of tobacco. He paid for it mechanically, and as he did so, the

Mexican flipped the stub of his cheroot into the gutter and began to move across the street.

Blossom watched him cross to the opposite sidewalk and pause in front of the *Painted Heifer*. Then, instead of entering the place he turned left and began to meander along. He did not seem in a hurry to get to any place in particular although he did seem to be glancing around him quite a bit – although that might only be the usual reactions of a man in a strange town.

Blossom left the store and crossed the street himself. He pretended to enter the saloon but only stood just inside the batwings, in the shade and watched the leisurely progress of his quarry.

The man went on and on…. Then, suddenly he vanished.

Blossom moved out into the street and began to walk along, trying to hurry without giving the appearance of doing so. The heels of his riding-boots made a hellish sound on the hollowness of the boardwalk. He slowed down as he reached the spot where the Mexican had vanished. It was as he expected. The man had slipped into one of the alleys that led to the 'backs' of Ridge Pleasant.

Maybe he was only doing a bit of exploring. But, now he had followed the man this far, Blossom was not inclined to give him the benefit of the doubt. He began to move up the alley.

He reached the top, and after removing his broad brimmed Stetson, peered around the corner. He had a confused glimpse of flashing legs in the distance, then the man had disappeared again. Blossom wasn't even sure whether he had really seen him or whether it had been just a trick of the sun.

He turned the corner and began to move along

the backs of the buildings, among the ashcans and the rubbish-dumps, and the sagging outhouses and privies. He nodded feebly to a housewife who peered at him through her kitchen window. What the hell was he doing prowling around here anyway? Like a durned alley-cat! The Mexican was probably back on the street again now, unimpressed by his view of Ridge Pleasant's domestic squalor.

Although Blossom did not want to over-play his hand, natural doggedness kept him going, moving nonchalantly around the outhouses, always keeping as close as possible to cover. Pretty soon he was behind the *Painted Heifer* with its cluster of outhouses, larger and in better repair than its neighbours! Its private stables, its small barn, its store-sheds and privies.

He was facing the small back door, the private entrance to Frank Heinkel's apartment when it opened and the Mexican came out. Blossom dodged into the open doorway of the barn and hoped the man had not spotted him.

The latter came on, hurrying now. He passed the door of the barn and Blossom stepped out behind him.

'Halt a minute, amigo,' he said.

The man turned with catlike grace. No hint of surprise showed on his rather bovine Latin face. He said with a tiny interrogative lift of his eyebrows.

'Yes, señor?'

Blossom flashed his badge and said, 'I'm from the sheriff's office. I'd like a few words with you.'

The greaser's shrug was almost on level with his thick black eyebrows. He said:

'But I have done notheenk, señor.'

'I didn't say you had. It's just that we're checking

up on strangers in town an' I'd like to ask you a few questions.'

The man shrugged again. 'So be it,' he said.

Blossom pointed. 'That way.' The man moved on in front of him around the corner of the barn. He went round the corner quickly, then whirled on his heels. Even the wide-awake young ex-gambler was taken by surprise as the man's knee came up and hit him in the pit of his stomach. He gulped and jack-knifed, reaching for his gun.

But the Mex had the inside edge now; his hand lifted, metal glinted in the sunlight. Blossom threw up his arm to ward off the blow but he was not quick enough. The gun-barrel descended with stunning force, smashing the crown of his Stetson. The world spun in fire around, then became suddenly very, very still. He hit the floor with his face but he did not feel anything any more.

When he came around he was lying on a pile of straw inside the barn. His hat lay beside him. There was a lump as big as a duck egg on the back of his head.

He rose and staggered to the door. He leaned on the jamb and dragged great gulps of air into his lungs. Gradually his head ceased to spin, the sensation was replaced by a dull burning ache. An irritating ache which made him feel murderous. Fancy trying to talk to a snaky specimen like that greaser without first of all poking a gun into his back. A slick lawman he had turned out to be and no mistake!

He went out of the barn and down an alley into the street. There was hardly anybody around and no signs of the flashy Mexican. As if there would be! The snaky buzzard was probably streaking for parts unknown right now.

But Blossom's experience had not been altogether a dead loss. A closer inspection of the man's clothing during the short time they had faced each other had allowed Blossom to ascertain the fact that the silver charms on the man's vest were identical to the one he had found out in the badlands. Further more, there had been a gap in the shining row. Blossom's quick gambling eyes had allowed him to learn this much but they had not been quick enough to allow him to prevent the sidewinder's lightning treachery.

So that man had something to do with the dead man in the desert! Maybe something to do with the outlaw gang! Then what had he been doing on Frank Heinkel's backstairs?

Blossom retraced his steps and entered the back door. He climbed the stairs and tried the door at the top. As usual it was locked and bolted on the inside. He thumped on the panels hard, and waited. There was no answer.

He retraced his steps once more, went on to the main drag and into the main entrance of the saloon. He said 'Hi-yuh' to the barman, climbed the stairs, went along to Heinkel's apartment at the end of the passage. He knocked, waited, knocked again. There was no answer so he tried the door. It was locked.

He heard another door open and turned. Dulcie stood in the passage.

She said, 'I think uncle's gone out.' Then she disappeared again. The door closed behind her.

Blossom walked down the passage, hesitated outside the closed door, then with a little shrug, passed on.

He went downstairs and from the barman ascertained the fact that the boss had indeed ridden out – about ten minutes ago.

He climbed the stairs again and went to his own room. Where was he now? Up a prickly pear tree! Had Heinkel's absence anything to do with the Mexican? Maybe Heinkel had not seen the man – maybe the Mex had gone up the stairs with robbery in mind, and finding the door barred, had given it up as a bad job. Maybe it was just a coincidence Heinkel riding out right afterwards like that. Blossom could not imagine the connection between the intelligent, reserved saloon-owner and the garish Mexican.

He bathed his head with icy-cold water and took savage pleasure in the pain it caused him. He'd damwell asked for it, hadn't he?

ELEVEN

As Frank Heinkel sent his horse at a gallop towards Sundown his thoughts were mixed. What was this news Mancey had for him? Could it be anything else but good news? The news he had been waiting for! Only untold wealth could soften the bitterness that had grown in him these last few days – could help Dulcie to forget her grief which he himself had, unwittingly, caused her. Maybe after this ride they could get away from Ridge Pleasant, to the ranch he had always promised her. She must never be allowed to suspect.

All the time, while his mind played with these thoughts, at the back of it was a dull dread. What had happened to Duke Pitson? Was he alive or dead? What did *he* now, in the light of his new-found knowledge, want for Duke Pitson?

He reached Sundown and went right in to Mancey. The thin man came out from behind his desk and shook hands ceremoniously.

But this time Heinkel had little time for politeness. He said tersely:

'It was a fool trick to send Juan after me.'

'I wanted to see you quickly.'

'Why? Is it good news about the Zack Mowbray job?' Heinkel sat down.

Mancey Cole went back behind his desk and seated himself before he answered.

'No. I fear that was a mare's nest. We found the seam but it was a false one. We got a few ounces of dust then it petered out altogether.'

Heinkel laughed bitterly. 'I might've known that old buzzard would never make a lucky strike.' Then his voice became sharp again. His usual composure seemed to be deserting him. He snapped:

'What is it then? You didn't bring me all the way here to tell me you *haven't* found any gold.'

'We've got a prisoner.'

'A prisoner?'

'Yes. Your esteemed friend, Sheriff Pitson.'

Heinkel could not conceal his surprise. 'How?'

Mancey told him the full tale. Then Heinkel said:

'I thought I had killed him. I hit him as hard as I could and he fell down that cleft. I wonder if he knows.'

'Somehow I don't think he does.'

Heinkel was at a loss. Always the boss previously, the cool schemer, he now almost unconsciously handed over the initiative to the other man. 'What shall we do?'

'I have a plan. A rather amusing plan.'

'All right. Let's have it.'

'The sheriff is very, very popular in Ridge Pleasant is he not?'

'He is.'

'Would they be prepared to collect – say five thousand dollars – among themselves in order to ensure his safe return?'

'What in tarnation are you getting at?'

'Ransom,' said Mancey with a little smile. 'Hold the sheriff to ransom....'

'And let him free afterwards so that he can start all over...?'

'No, of course not. As soon as we receive the money we can finish him off. We can manage that somehow. It will be the answer to our problem – and we shall be better off by five thousand dollars. The whole thing could be engineered just by you and I – nobody else to share with. What do you think of that?'

'It sounds all right.' But Heinkel still looked a little doubtful.

'The question is: do the townsfolk love their law-officer that much?' said Mancey.

'I don't know,' Heinkel looked up. 'Is the sheriff all right?'

'Yes, he's in good health. He's in the old dungeon.'

'I'll go and have a peep at him through the grill before I go. I'll sound things out back in town and let you know my final decision tomorrow.'

'All right,' said Mancey.

Duke Pitson lay on his back on a heap of damp straw in the corner of the old dungeon. The walls were crumbling and running with moisture. There were creeping things on the surface, and in another corner, a family of bullfrogs kept up their monotonous baritone warbling. The door was reached by a short flight of steps. Duke knew it was made of logs about a foot thick and was barred on the other side. There was no window but, high in the wall directly opposite the door, was a small iron-barred grill. Not much light filtered through there; the place was gloomy, the air was clammy and there was a nauseating stench.

Duke was no believer in miracles. Consequently, when something akin to one suddenly happened he was leary. Things like this just didn't happen! It must be a trick of some kind!

He picked up the small, double-barrelled derringer which had clattered as it fell through the grill. He looked up. The walls, the gleaming iron bars, they told him nothing. He inspected the derringer. It was fully loaded…. Maybe his captors wanted him to shoot himself to save themselves the trouble. He smiled wryly. No, they could hardly be that simple. And such as they could have no humane feelings. There must be some other reason for the sudden appearance of this deadly little weapon.

Maybe he had a friend in the camp after all. Somebody who wanted him to have a chance to escape? Somebody from Ridge Pleasant perhaps – the spy? Maybe a man who he called friend – who had been leading a double life. This was fantasy! Or maybe it was hope – a forlorn one…. If it was trickery after all – well, he'd take a chance on that. You only lived once!…

So it was the gaoler, balancing a tray in one hand, and his gun in the other, deceived by the shape of something on the straw in the dim corner, marched boldly in. And stopped, transfixed, as the muzzle of a gun was poked into his back. He did not stop to wonder how the prisoner had gotten hold of the weapon. He knew the cold hard feel of the thing and made no protest when his own gun was wrenched from his fingers.

'Put the tray down on the floor,' said a voice that sent shivers up and down the man's back. 'Gently now; you don't want to die yet do yuh?'

The gaoler bent and did as ordered.

'March,' said the voice. 'Don't tread on the tray now.'

The gaoler skirted the tray and marched. As he got nearer to the corner he realised that what had looked to him like a man was merely a man's vest stuffed with straw. After that he did not wonder any more for a vicious blow sent him sprawling on his face, unconscious.

Duke retrieved his vest and put it on. He draped the gaoler artistically in its place. The man would snooze for quite a while. With his scalp split open like that he might even die. Duke did not give it another thought but cat-footed across the cell and out of it. He closed the door gently behind him.

He was in a stone passage, the crumbling walls unbroken by any window or door. He sped along, very light-footed for all his bulk. The passage had a corner at the end. He flattened himself against the wall and listened.

He stuck his head around the corner. His body followed it sinuously. He climbed a flight of stone steps to another door. He opened it a crack and peered out.

In front of him was a long hall ranged by high windows through which the sun poured in golden streams. The place was high and vaulted and had a cathedral-like appearance marred only by the fact that the floor was strewn haphazardly with rough tables and benches. The mess-room and assembly hall no doubt, figured Duke. And empty too.

Directly opposite him was another door, a double

one beneath an archway. One wing of it was open. There was blackness beyond.

The hall seemed to be a mile wide. Duke's body was as tense as a bow-string as he began to cross it. Although he tried to tip-toe, his boots awoke the echoes in the high vaulted place. He choked back an impulse to run. He skirted the tables and chairs gingerly. He was transfixed by hot sunshine streaming through the glassless windows and the sweat began to break out on his face.

He was three-parts of the way across the floor and was beginning to feel a sense of relief when a fat man came through the open door. He was whistling between his teeth and did not at first see Duke.

There was nothing else for it. Even as the man's eyes bulged and his mouth opened, Duke fired from the hip.

The man gave a queer little gulp and clutched at his stomach. He was a writhing bundle on the floor when the big red-head leapt over him and streaked for the door.

He found himself in a kind of porch. There was a closed door opposite. He turned the heavy iron ring in its middle and pulled. It opened. He looked out quickly. Then he moved out, closing the door behind him. He was in a courtyard facing a brokendown pile of out-houses. The back of the hacienda he figured. The wall was crumbling and had many gaps. The courtyard was empty.

There was the way to freedom. But he could not take it on foot. He had to have a horse. He moved swiftly along the wall to a corner and looked around. There were sounds as well as sight now. Horses; about two hundred yards from him. But men there too. Four of them. Standing and smoking. Looking as if they were billeted there in comradeship for some considerable time.

To face that number would be suicide. They would draw as soon as they saw him. One consolation was that they evidently hadn't heard the shot from the mess-room.

His only hope seemed to be in getting to the opposite corner which was directly at their side, and taking them by surprise. To do that he would have to go all the way round the mess-room. The thought of doing that and maybe running into trouble the other side when escape had seemed so near was almost unbearable. He thought of negotiating the wall and taking a chance on a horse among the huts outside the hacienda. But that was too risky. With every minute the danger of the discovery of the shot man inside was becoming more eminent. Horses he could see and one of those horses he must have!

He began to retrace his steps. Back past the door he had recently quitted, moving along the wall, a fly in the sunlight, a target for anybody who looked over that crumbing wall opposite.

It was not only the heat that was making the sweat start from his body when he reached the other corner. It seemed to him that everybody in the vicinity must have heard his hurried footsteps.

He peeped around the corner and almost shouted at what he saw. His luck had caught up with him at last! There was a horse, a big, black fast-looking beast. A man was grooming it and his back was towards Duke.

The red-headed lawman did not waste any more time but began to move forward. He was almost upon his quarry when the fellow turned. A yell escaped his lips and he went for his gun. Duke, chary of risking another shot, did the next best thing. He swung a long leg and kicked the crouching man under the jaw.

There was a sickening crunching sound and the wretch went over backwards. His head was at a queer angle, his eyes staring upwards as Duke clapped a nearby saddle blanket on to the bare back of the horse then forked it.

As soon as his heels touched the beast's flanks it began to move. Duke gave it another double kick and it soared over the wall. He could feel the rippling power of its body beneath him. He was lucky in landing in the least populated area of the settlement. Just a few huts, from one of which a man came running, shouting, a gun in his hand. Duke took a pot-shot at him and he ducked into cover and began to blaze away.

The shots terrified the horse and goaded him to a fresh burst of speed.

A couple of slugs whistled near the man's head then there were no more. He swerved his mount, hoping he was going in roughly the right direction, and they sped on.

He was jubilant. With a magnificent piece of horseflesh like this beneath him they could not catch him now. But how he wished he had a proper saddle and a pair of reins!

When Mancey Cole heard of the escape of his valuable prisoner he flew into one of his rare rages. But when they told him that the lawman must have gotten a gun from someplace he became suddenly strangely silent. When he spoke he asked that two men called Bat and Clarence should be sent to him.

The two men came. Bat was big and very ugly. His enormous ears were a blatant indication of the source of his nickname. Clarence was a thin stooping gent with eyes like green marbles. He looked the essence of malignity.

Mancey, with his usual charming forthrightness, went to the point right away.

'Nobody in Ridge Pleasant knows you two, do they?'

Both men confessed to never having been there.

'But you know it?'

They knew it. 'And you weren't in on the bank-raid. I don't think even Heinkel knows you very well.' Mancey paused. Then he went on decisively. 'I want you to ride to Ridge Pleasant and get that damn sheriff and his pard, Frank Heinkel....'

'Frank Heinkel?'

'Don't you like the idea?'

Bat grinned. 'I like it all right,' he said. 'It's about time that panty-waist was taken care of. We'd sooner have you for boss.'

'All right! Do as I say. I don't care how you do it but do it properly and don't lead anybody here on your tail. There'll be a big fee for both of you I can promise you that.'

'Leave it to us, Mancey,' said the green-eyed Clarence. His voice was like the purr of a cat.

'All right. Get going!'

It was twilight in Ridge Pleasant. The quiet time before the bawdy night. The bar-room of the *Painted Heifer* was almost empty.

Duke Pitson was back, risen miraculously from the dead, and had received the ovations of the townsfolk with his usual calm although, if truth be known, he was rather touched by it all.

Form her window Dulcie had seen him arrive. She was standing at the top of the stairs waiting for him as he limped across the bar-room. One look at her shining face had told him all he wanted to know.

Neither of them spoke but there were tears in her eyes as she led him along the passage and into her room.

Nobody knew what passed in there but when Duke came downstairs again, freshly dressed and groomed, a plastered swab on his head, he walked like a man who was bursting with new-found joy. Although his face looked the same there was something in his eyes and irradiating from him that was different. There was a purpose there too. He was a reincarnated and whole man, except for that slight limp.

Frank Heinkel was nowhere around; the barman said he had gone down the street. He owned a few more places in Ridge Pleasant. Maybe he was paying them one of his rare visits. Duke decided to go down to the gaol and startle the boys.

He was making for the batwings when Blossom came in. The dark young ex-gambler had at long last given up Duke as irrevocably lost, consequently he could not conceal his utter astonishment at seeing his friend there waiting for him. And in much better condition, seemingly than the travel-stained Blossom himself.

His poker-face crumpled alarmingly, his mouth fled open. Duke strode forward and grasped his hand but it was some seconds before the young man could articulate his friend's name.

Duke led him over to a table in a quiet corner and sat him down. He began to tell his tale, and as it progressed Blossom's face became tense.

Afterwards he had something to say too. Chief among his news, and the most puzzling part about it, was the recollection of Frank Heinkel's strange and treacherous visitor.

Duke listened him out and began to put two and two together. They made a very shaky three, probably because he fought unconsciously against making them anything else.

The Mexican with the charms on his clothes. There was little doubt in either of the men's minds that he was a member of the outlaw band. His treachery when confronted by a lawman seemed to bear out that fact. Then what had he been doing on the backstairs of Frank Heinkel's apartment? Had his motive been robbery? – or something else? Then there was the fact of the gun dropped into Duke's cell back in Sundown. Guns did not drop from the sky in some miraculous way! And Frank had been doing a lot of private riding of his, at all sorts of odd times. According to the barman he had returned only just before the reincarnated law-officer rode in. After stabling his horse he had gone almost immediately for a walk down the street.... No, he didn't look any different than usual.

There was no use in jumping to conclusions. If the saloon-owner had any connection with the bandit gang whatsoever, maybe it was not of his own choosing. Maybe they had found some means of blackmailing him. Duke hoped for Heinkel's sake, as well as Dulcie's that, were his suspicions founded in fact, there would be some extenuating circumstances. The thought of Dulcie sent a sharp stab to his heart. He felt like a dog in a treadmill must have felt, going round and round and round to little purpose.

He said: 'We'd better let things ride for a bit. As soon as the folks start coming in here I'm gonna call for a posse. We've got to get to Sundown pronto before the birds take it into their heads to fly. But I've got to see Heinkel.'

Blossom rose. 'I'll go and get myself cleaned up.'
He climbed the stairs.

Duke was crossing to the bar to get himself
another drink when Frank Heinkel came in. The
lawman was half-turned away from the batwings so he
did not see the other man's first reactions.

He turned to see Heinkel's lined face lit by one of
his rare gentle smiles. He came forward, hand
outstretched.

'I told them you were all right, Duke,' he said. 'I
told them!'

Duke took the thin hand. It was engulfed by his
own but the grip was firm and strong. Could this
gentle-seeming gent from whom, in their five odd
years association together he had experienced only
courtesy and friendship, have anything to do with
that hell's brew in the badlands?

They leaned on the bar and he told his story, just
the way he had told it to Blossom. Outside it was
almost completely dusk but as yet the barman had
not lit all the lamps and the bar-room was a quiet
place of shadows with pools of light here and there.

Duke had almost finished his story when the diversion occurred. The two strangers came through the
batwings, one behind the other. They did not
however seem to be together. The big one angled off
to the right a piece, the crook-backed one to the left.

Maybe Duke was particularly sensitive after his
recent action-full experiences. He thought he felt
Heinkel stiffen beside him. The short hairs began to
prickle on the big man's neck and he knew that
something was going to happen.

The two men came on, making for the bar. They
glanced at each other then, as if a signal had passed
between them they began to move. But Duke had

been watching their eyes and he moved too – yelling a warning to Heinkel, throwing his body sideways in a lop-sided crouch as he went for his guns.

He concentrated on the evil-looking stooping man first, knowing without a doubt that he was a worthy opponent. The latter had the inside edge, a fraction of time gained while Duke was yelling and moving. But his first shot shattered a bottle behind Duke's head. Then through a haze of powder-smoke the big man was thumbing the hammers of his Colt.

Like wisps of cloud moving aside the smoke cleared and the lean man was crumpling, letting his guns go so that they clattered to the floor a split-second before his crooked body followed them.

The big man was swaying, trying to bring his gun level. Duke fired two more shots, aiming at the broad chest, watching little puffs of dust spurt from there as the big body shook. It crashed to the floor.

Duke turned slowly. He felt infinitely weary. He looked down at Frank Heinkel, sprawled at his feet, his bare head propped up against the bar, one thin hand clutching the brass footrail. The dark eyes implored him and Heinkel said:

'Duke – come closer – quickly....'

Duke went down on his knees beside him, noting with a slow sadness the spreading red stain on the immaculate shirt front, the glow fading from the dark eyes. He knew it was useless to touch the man. Heinkel spoke in staccato phrases, weak between tearing gasps. His knuckles on the footrail were like polished bone. He was hanging on tenaciously to life itself until he knew it was time for him to go.

'Two of the boys.... I guess Mancey sent them to get us.... I worked with the gang.... Sundown.... Gave them information, planned their jobs.... I – I wanted Dulcie to have everything…. Believe that, Duke – believe that….' The fading eyes implored again.

'I believe it,' said Duke, softly.

'I slugged you in the hills…. fired the three alarm shots in order to warn the Sundowners…. I was sorry – sorry…. I've been wrong all along…. wrong….' His voice faded.

'Frank,' said Duke urgently. 'Frank.'

The eyes brightened a little again as the dying man made a super-human effort. The voice went on.

'I'd tried to make it up…. dropped the Derringer into the dungeon….' He coughed and a red line of frothy blood ran down his chin. Duke took out a handkerchief and gently wiped it away. The voice became spasmodic, yet seemingly more powerful, a last spurt of brilliance before the flame died.

'Git Mancey Cole…. The money from the bank-robbery…. waterproof bag…. in old well…. middle of hacienda…. I – I….'

The words ended in a hoarse rattle and for a second the face was contorted. Then it became peaceful, the eyes closed, that little gentle smile on the lips once more. So Frank Heinkel died.

TWELVE

The shooting had brought folks a-running. Dulcie came downstairs as her uncle died. She was stunned. Grief – joy – now grief again. It was almost unbearable. She looked to Duke piteously for guidance.

He, thankful that she had not heard her uncle's last words and resolved that she never would know the truth of them, knew that only more blood could wipe the slate clean. As men carried the shell of her uncle up to his room he told the girl gently what he must do. She was sturdy frontier stock, ashamed now of her moment of weakness. She elected to go back upstairs to watch over her uncle and await her lover's return.

He escorted her to her room and kissed her gently before he left.

When he returned to the bar-room they were all waiting for him. Silently, their faces upturned as he came down the stairs. He did not waste words.

There was a call for 'horses, horses,' and as he moved amid the mêlée, he saw Milo Platt. They exchanged glances, neither them revealing the fact that they were anything more than acquaintances.

Milo came nearer and said: 'I'm kind of a stranger hereabout, Sheriff, but I'd certainly like to be in on this shindig.'

Duke bowed slightly. 'We need fighting men of your calibre, Mr Platt,' he said.

For a moment he reflected cynically that maybe the marshal only wanted to come along in order to keep an eye on his quarry. But maybe he was being unfair! Milo was the kind of a man who lived for excitement and the chance to put his prowess to the test. Maybe he was getting bored with waiting too.

Inside the half-hour the cavalcade began to ride. A larger bunch of grim, vengeful fighting men had never set out from Ridge Pleasant before, and they left behind them many fluttering and anxious female hearts. At the head rode their leader, Duke Pitson. With him the inscrutable Blossom, the lean tow-headed Gil, the dour Brock. And strangest of all, though looking quite in place, the tall, willowy young-old man with the cold eyes who called himself Milo Platt and was reputed to be a notorious gun-fighter from down south.

It was a dark still night and though the moon was in existence it was fighting a losing battle against ranks of ponderous clouds.

Out on the badlands Duke halted his men. From there they could not even see the ghost-town. They had no means of knowing whether it had been evacuated or not.

Duke proposed that he and Blossom, the greatest tracker of them all, should go forward and investigate.

'Give us ten minutes,' he said. 'Then spread out and begin to move slowly in. We'll either come out again to meet you or fire three shots. If you hear three shots attack immediately. Look out for Blossom an' myself – we don't want none of yuh to put a slug in either of us.'

The two men moved on, and after a moment, Duke veered his horse, saying: 'We'll make a detour here – try to get in the back of the place where I came out earlier today.'

'D'yuh think they'll be waiting for us?'

'I don't know. I think they'll be there anyway. They've hardly had time to get clean away. Anyway, I guess they think they're pretty safe in their little fortress. This is how I figure it…. Mancey Cole must have had plenty of faith in the efficiency of those two gun-slingers. He probably thinks by now that Heinkel and I have both cashed in our checks and his men are on their way back. I guess he didn't take into account their arrogance, their assumption that they could take us both across a floor. That was their mistake – and his. Neither of them was *quite* fast enough….'

The moon broke its way through the clouds for a second, lighting the plain before them, and they saw the eerie cluster of buildings that was Sundown.

A few minutes later they were moving again in blackness when the big man said:

'We should be around the side of the place now. A bit farther an' we'll trust to luck an' start to move in.'

'Something tells me this is about it,' said Blossom a few moments later.

That uncanny sense of his had not played him false for, suddenly, the crumbling wall loomed up out of the blackness before them. Here there were no huts.

'Hold it,' hissed the young man. 'There's some-body there.'

Beyond the wall was a faint diffused light. Duke followed with his eyes the direction of Blossom's pointing finger and saw, faintly outlined above the tortured shape of the wall, the head and shoulders of a man.

The big man expelled a deep breath. If that galoot saw them they were sunk. He thought fast, jerked his head, and turning his horse's head, began to ride slowly parallel with the wall. A bit farther along they saw the red pin-point of a cigarette. Another sentinel. They turned and rode back a piece. Then they left their horses and proceeded forward again on foot. Duke unhooked his *riata* from his saddle pommel.

'We'll take the right-hand one first,' whispered Duke.

They reached the extreme end of the wall without mishap and began to move along in its shadows. It seemed like there were no gaps this end, until they got to the sentinel. It looked like they would have to attack him from the outside. If they attempted to climb the wall he was liable to spot them.

They formulated a plan. It was risky but seemed the only one that would work in the circumstances.

They were almost upon the man. Duke rose and sauntered immediately in front of him. He knew he was taking a big risk but he banked on the fact that the man would at first think him a member of the gang having a constitutional.

The man followed him with his eyes. Astonishment seemed to temporarily paralyse him. Then he said, 'Hey?' And Blossom sprang.

He came out of the shadows like a mountain-cat. His arm crooked around the guard's throat, choking off his cry. They sank to the ground together, the guard gurgling horribly. Duke flattened himself against the wall and kept a look out. He knew Blossom didn't need any help. He had seen his Indian-like savagery at work before.

Finally there was no more sound from the guard and Blossom hissed, 'All right.'

Duke strode over the wall and joined him. They were inside the outer ring of the fortress and there was nobody else in sight. But, to be on the safe side, they had to take care of that other guard. They moved slowly along in the shadows once more.

It was easy this time. A stealthy approach, a swinging gun. Duke caught the unconscious man as he fell. He would sleep sound. At least he was better off than his comrade, if Duke knew anything of Blossom's methods.

They began to move forward among 'dobe huts and crumbling shacks. They came suddenly upon another man. He did not even have time to open his mouth. A slashing gun-barrel tore into his face and he went over backwards without a sound. The marauders had no time for niceties.

The light streamed from the windows of the assembly hall. The space at the side was empty except for three horses. They crept to a window and even Duke had to crane his neck to see above the high sill.

About thirty men were gathered there. They were eating, drinking, playing cards, dicing. A few of them were sunk in drunken sleep with their heads on the tables.

Duke evolved a desperate plan. He told it to Blossom, and the young man, who had been taking chances all his life, raised no objection. They moved around to the heavy front door, which Duke had learned during his short sojourn there, was the place's only exit. The back door led only to the dungeons.

While Blossom kept watch outside, Duke, carrying his coiled *riata*, went through the outer door and across the deserted porch. The other door was ajar and through it came the sound of revelry. He closed it gently. He unwound a length of his *riata* and tied the end to the door-handle. Then he began to play out the rope as he backed away.

Still uncoiling the forty-foot rope he joined Blossom. The latter followed him as he went round the corner of the building. He lashed what was left of the rope to a convenient buttress, one of the many niceties with which the crumbling place was adorned, broken reminders of its old magnificence.

The two men helped themselves to a couple of the horses which stood nearby. Then, leading the beasts, they parted.

Duke did not go far. He mounted the horse and eased it over to one of the windows. He knew Blossom would be doing the same the other side. He leaned against the wall so that he could not be seen from the inside and quickly checked over his guns. Then he peered into the place.

He could not see Mancey Cole in there. He had not expected to somehow. The buzzard could wait awhile.

It was his job to fire the three shots that would be the signal for the band outside. He resolved that those three slugs would not be wasted. He picked his men, raised his guns and let fly.

Three men fell as if they had been stricken down by a thunderbolt. Surprise turned the assembled company to statues. Then Blossom opened up. He did not waste any shots either.

Pandemonium broke loose as men sought cover, dragging their guns and attempting to retaliate at the death-dealing creatures whom they could not see in the blackness outside.

Some ran to the door, only to find that tug as they might they could not budge it. One man was transfixed there like a crushed fly and fell slowly to a crumpled heap at the threshold.

For a time it was systematic slaughter as Blossom and Duke, remembering many bitter things, poured lead mercilessly into the glaring amphitheatre and shot to kill each time. Then a small band of the men entrenched themselves behind an upturned table in a corner. Others opened the back door and fled to the dungeons…. Then somebody shot the lights out.

There was a lull in the firing and Duke heard more gunshots a distance away and knew that his men had attacked. He rode his horse away from the window and around to Blossom, who had stopped to reload.

He said: 'The boys are attacking. It sounds like they're meeting opposition. I want to try and get behind those bozoes. I also want to get Mancey Cole….'

'I'll stay here an' keep this lot busy if you like,' said Blossom.

For a fraction of time Duke hesitated. Then he said, 'All right. But don't take any chances. Pull from under if it gets too hot.'

Blossom nodded. Already he was turning his head and shooting again. Duke left him and rode in the direction of the other shots. They were cracking now like a Fourth of July display and pretty soon he could see the flashes.

He reached the main ruins of the hacienda,

dismounted from his horse, and began to move around the wall. As he reached the front door he realised the enemy were entrenched behind the wall opposite and around the gateway. They must have retreated there. The night was hideous with gunfire and shouting voices.

He was in the shadows beside the door when it opened and a man came out. A gun glinted in his hand. Duke swung his own weapon down in a vicious arc. It hit the man's wrist and he screamed as the bone snapped. Then Duke was upon him, forcing him back through the door.

He raised his hands to shield his face as the gun-barrel descended again. The heavy steel smashed his fingers, plunged on, tore a groove in his cheek. He went down on his knees in the passage.

Duke put the sole of his boot against the man's chest and forced him on to his back. The man tried to cover up again. There was stark terror in the eyes above the bleeding hands.

Duke bent over him. 'Where's Mancey Cole?'

The man jerked his head feebly, pointing down the passage.

'Sorry, pardner,' said Duke and stunned him with another blow across the temple.

He went down the passage. He remembered it well now. This was where they had brought him first of all after he was captured. Cole's room was just around the corner.

The corridor was deserted, lit by the meagre light of a single lantern in the roof. Duke approached the room on tiptoes. Light showed beneath the door. He turned the handle gently. The door was locked. The light went out suddenly. There was utter ominous silence.

Duke went back along the passage, reached up a long arm and unhooked the lantern from the ceiling. Then with gun in one hand and lantern in the other he retraced his steps.

He stood a little to the side of the door and smashed the lock with two swift shots. The door swung gently in powder-smoke. He kicked the door wide open, throwing himself backwards as he flung the lantern.

Slugs made a pattern on the opposite wall as the man inside opened up. Then Duke heard him cry out in agony. The big man took a chance and dived in.

Mancey Cole was transfixed in a ruddy light. There was paper money all around him. Some of it was on fire and Cole's sleeve was burning too as he tried to save the precious stuff. He screamed at Duke, raising the gun in his other hand.

The sheriff of Ridge Pleasant fired coolly, twice, and watched the other man sink below the level of the table, the clawing fingers still raking at the money until, as if reluctant to let go, they finally disappeared from sight.

He had evidently been cramming the greenbacks into the open saddle-bag on the table. Duke began to beat at the burning bills himself. It was good money and it belonged to Ridge Pleasant. He crammed both the saddle-bags full of the stuff. Not much of it was destroyed. He felt bitterness, reflecting how much tragedy these sheafs of green paper had caused.

By the time he quitted the place the furniture was on fire and the body of Mancey Cole was a blazing pyre. He would not feel anything. He had died more quickly than he deserved.

Duke flung the bulging saddle-bags over his shoulder and went down the corridor, through the door. There was fighting going on out there. The Ridge Pleasant men had left their horses and were moving in.

A bunch of the enemy were backing towards the doorway when Duke strode through it. With his arms free now he could use both guns again. He did so – with terrible effect. Men went down like chaff before a hail of lead from this demon gun-fighter, who seemed to have materialised from nowhere.

Duke yelled. 'Keep moving, boys! Keep moving!'

A slug plucked at his sleeve and he whirled, going down on one knee, slamming the hammer of his Colt. The attacker ducked then turned and ran. Somebody else fired across the yard and the man seemed to stumble. Then he pitched forward on his face.

Bobbing and weaving, Gil ran across the yard, beside him Brock. The latter's knee suddenly went from under him and he crumpled up. Gil caught him. They were a target there in the open. A bunch of the enemy were entrenched behind an upturned cart. Duke probably had a better view of them than anybody. Still kneeling, he dropped one gun on the ground beside him, and fanning the hammer of the other, sent a stream of lead across the yard. Covered for a time Gil dragged Brock across into the shadows of the wall.

Duke backed and joined them. For the moment the enemy let them be. They were concentrating on the others, who were advancing in ever-increasing numbers. There were still pockets of resistance, but they were scattered, men hugging cover as they fought desperately.

Brock's wound proved to be only a flesh one near

his hip. Duke left him there with Gil, and suddenly fearful of the safety of his sidekick, ran in the direction of the assembly hall. As he turned the corner he looked back. The bandits had suddenly given up hope and were streaming from hiding-places with their hands above their heads. Men ran towards Duke. The one in front was Milo Platt.

'You all right, Sheriff?' he said.

Duke nodded his head. 'Come on,' he said. 'We haven't finished yet.'

The men, about a couple of dozen of them now, followed him. Behind them the rest were getting the beaten foe roped-up. The flames from the burning hacienda threw an ever-widening aura of light and made their task easier.

Firing was still going on at the assembly hall. The sound of it was like sweet music. It told Duke that Blossom was still holding his own.

The younker was still on his perch, firing with one gun. His other arm, dripping with blood, hung lax beside him. He turned and grinned at their approach. Then they caught him as he slumped in a dead faint.

'What sheer guts,' said Milo softly. 'He must have lost pints of blood.'

Duke climbed on to the horse's back in Blossom's stead. Inside the shooting had died down. He shouted:

'Listen, you people. The place is surrounded and the rest of your partners have given in. The hacienda is on fire. We'll give you three minutes to throw down your arms and come out. If you don't we're gonna set this place alight too. Start to throw your guns through the window!'

He had hardly finished speaking before the

weapons began to thud to the ground outside.

With that the last spark of resistance was squashed. There were so many prisoners that many of them had to be locked up in the dungeons under four guards until other accommodation could be found for them.

It was the following morning. A peaceful sunny morning and Ridge Pleasant was licking its wounds. They were miraculously light ones. There was only one death. That of Jamesey Porter the gunsmith. He had been a popular man, but fortunately, had no dependants. There was quite a crop of wounds but nothing very serious.

The townsfolk mourned for Frank Heinkel and Jamesey, and rubbed their hands secretly the while because they had gotten their money back.

Duke Pitson was the hero of the hour but what he thought about that nobody knew. He had ceased to be a fighting-machine and was the inscrutable gent once more. He had even taken back his broadcloth and his fancy waistcoat. He had not resigned his post as sheriff but that was expected to be his next move. Things certainly were pointing that way but nobody seemed to be able to get near enough to Duke to sound him out. He spent most of his time with Dulcie. When they were together, even if there were other people around, it seemed like there was nobody else in the world but them.

That morning up in Dulcie's room nobody could see them. They were sitting at the window and Duke pointed downwards to Milo Platt, who was lounging with a cigarette in his mouth at the hitching-rack below. He began to tell Dulcie a story.

It was about a big-shot gambler who ran a faro-layout in a big luxurious honky-tonk in a southern town. He had a young assistant who was also his bosom friend. He had another friend, the marshal of the town, a proud, quick-tempered gent. This marshal had a bosom friend, too, his half-brother who was also his deputy. This half-brother was the weak link in this chain. He was a drunkard and a gambler who never knew when he'd had enough of anything. He used his office to his own ends and was quick to use his guns if he had the inside edge. He pleaded the law over the dead body of many a cowboy whose only sin had been high spirits.

He hated the big-shot gambler and the gambler hated him. Things came to a head one night when the deputy marshal was bucking the tiger at the faro-bank. He lost and he kept losing, and finally he flew into a rage, accused the gambler of cheating, and went for his gun. The gambler shot it from his hand, drove him from the place at gun-point, made him look a fool and a coward in front of everybody.

The following day the two men met on the street in the morning sunshine. Without warning the deputy drew his gun. He wounded the gambler in the arm and the gambler killed him. He was faster, much faster. He had always been the fastest shooting man in town – except maybe for the marshal who was his friend.

Now they were no longer friendly. The gambler had killed the deputy, the half-brother, and the law must take its revenge. The gambler had two courses open to him. Either he ran away or he faced and maybe killed his friend with whom he had no quarrel. He chose to leave and his assistant went with him.

Duke finished and Dulcie said:

'Your cynical way of telling this tale cannot

disguise the fact from me that you were the gambler and Blossom was your assistant.'

Duke nodded. Then he pointed downwards. 'And Milo Platt was the marshal – still is. I don't want to kill him, and even if I do, there'll be others. I can't keep on running. Particularly now I've got you. I made a bargain with Milo. I promised to go back with him as soon as my job was finished here. I've got to face the music. There are plenty of witnesses who'll testify that what I did was in self-defence – lawman or no lawman. I guess Milo meant to kill me, but now, even if he had the chance I don't think he'd take it. We were friends once you see and these things can't be forgotten....'

'He came all the way here to get revenge...?'

Duke shrugged. 'Revenge, duty, pride – call it what you will.'

When they looked through the window again Milo had moved out of sight. A few moments later the man and the girl went down the stairs together. A youth ran across the bar-room towards them. He waved an envelope.

'A gent tol' me to give yuh this, Sheriff,' he said.

Duke took it, extracted a sheet of paper. He unfolded it and read aloud the hurried scrawl:

''Dear Bill.... I lied when I said there was a price on your head. The case was closed, self defence, after you left. A man is never too old to learn, and fighting with you and your new friends yesterday I learnt a lot. You were right when you said revenge was not sweet. I dealt myself the wrong hand. I am turning it in now.

For the game, gracias. And adios amigo.

Milo.'

'Wait for me, Dulcie,' said Duke. 'I'll be back.'

He ran from the saloon, vaulted into the saddle of

the first horse he saw, and sent it thundering down the street.

At the end he reined in slowly and looked out on to the trail at the bobbing receding figure in the shimmering heat-haze. The figure seemed to pause, to grow a little taller. Then an arm was raised in salute.

A few moments later there was nothing but the sun and the dust and the magical haze. Duke turned his horse's head and rode slowly back.

Dulcie was waiting for him on the street of Ridge Pleasant. He had wandered far but now he was home .... home....